CALLS FOR SUBMISSION

by

SELENA CHAMBERS

Calls For Submission by Selena Chambers

ISBN: 978-1-938349-62-1
eISBN: 978-1-938349-67-6
Library of Congress Control Number: 2017932478

Cover Design by Joan Horne
Layout and Book Design by Mark Givens
Author Sketch by Yves Tourigny/www.yvestourigny.com

First Pelekinesis Printing 2017

For information:
Pelekinesis
112 Harvard Ave #65
Claremont, CA 91711 USA

www.pelekinesis.com

CALLS FOR SUBMISSION

* * *

SELENA CHAMBERS

To the Babes: Kat, Lori, Michelle, and Maureen.
You all inspired me to pick up the axe, and when
that didn't work out, the pen.

Praise for Selena Chambers

"Eerie and captivating—blissfully unnerving. Beautiful. Powerful. Selena Chambers is a radiant light among the foremost writers of horror and weird fiction working today. I am in awe of this lady's talent!"

—Joseph S. Pulver, Sr., editor of *The Madness of Dr. Caligari*

"Selena Chambers is a genuine spirit medium, and every story is a séance. Few fantasists are as versed in literary history, and none can summon up the decadent past as easily and as entertainingly."

—Nick Mamatas, author of *The Last Weekend* and *I Am Providence*

"I have always loved the richness of Selena Chambers' writing, and that richness is made even more apparent when her stories are gathered together in her collection, *Calls for Submission*. These stories are full of elegance and strangeness, written with a fierce intelligence that will haunt you. It's an excellent collection."

—Kat Howard, author of *Roses and Rot*

"Combining a welcome scholarly bent with a punk rock attitude, Selena Chambers pens tales as fresh as they are fierce. From suicidal Beat poets to alt-historical travelogues to a modern take on Poe's "M. Valdemar" (complete with rock bands), the stories in this brilliantly-titled debut may vary in tone, setting, and form, but they all share one thing in common: the unmistakable timbre of a resonant new voice in weird literature."

—Orrin Grey, author of *Painted Monsters & Other Strange Beasts*

"Selena Chambers's collection *Calls for Submission* is a wonderful, irresistible mix of the historical and modern, the literary and fantastic. These stories burst with humor, genuine emotion, wonder, and the dread of those who see the end coming."

—Paul Tremblay, author of *A Head Full of Ghosts* and *Disappearance at Devil's Rock*

"Selena Chambers is a rare visionary who is able to illuminate the poetry that lurks at the heart of the macabre. Her sumptuous prose and boundless imagination conjure a blazing pyre of souls, eras, worlds. I am in awe of her talent."

—Richard Gavin, author of *Sylvan Dread*

"From the dazzling mind of Selena Chambers, we are treated to fifteen provocative stories. Whether in collaboration with other writers, or on her own, her voice shines brightly through each tale. Although these stories have an underlying darkness within them, they are still gloriously illuminating."

—Ann VanderMeer, co-editor of *The Weird: A Compendium of Strange and Dark Stories* and *Sisters of the Revolution*.

"Reading Selena Chambers' fiction has the same unsettling sensation as walking into the waters of what you think is low tide—the sand is beneath your feet, the waters are warm and beautiful, all seems as a dream; and only when you have been lulled beyond the point of no return do you realize that you have stepped off into the deep, into a world stranger and more cruel and wondrous than you thought you'd been bargaining for. These are masterful and powerfully emotional stories that will lure you, enchant you, overwhelm you, and leave you gasping for air, and for more."

—Livia Llewellyn, author of *Furnace* and *Engines of Desire: Tales of Love & Other Horrors*

"Chambers' imagery and style almost induces synesthesia and reads as part homage to Poe and, more implicitly, to Rimbaud (and maybe even Burroughs)."

—PopMatters.com on "Dr. Lambshead's Dark Room"

"Gorgeous, intricately layered, and extremely strange, this piece may be the blue ribbon exhibit in an exemplary batch."

—*Locus Magazine*, on "The Neurastheniac."

"Of Parallel and Parcel" first appeared in *MungBeing* magazine, Issue #30: "Secrets." 2010.

"The Şehrazatın Diyoraması Tour" first appeared in *Steampunk World*, edited by Sarah Hans. Alliteration Ink. August 2014.

"Dr. Lambshead's Dark Room" first appeared in *The Thackery T. Lambshead Cabinet of Curiosities*. Harper Voyager. Edited by Ann and Jeff VanderMeer. July 2011.

"Descartar" first appeared in *The Darke Phantastique*. Cycatrix Press. Edited by Jason V. Brock. October 2014.

"Vintage Scenes #1: Bandol, Château La Rouvière, 2002" first appeared in *MungBeing* magazine, Issue #54: "New Direction." February 2014.

"Dive In Me" was co-authored with Jesse Bullington, and first appeared in *The New Gothic: Don't Embrace the Darkness. Fear It*, edited by Beth K. Lewis. Stone Skin Press. January 2014.

"Collaborative Disambiguation" was written with Virginia M. Mohlere and first appeared in *MungBeing* magazine, Issue 12: "Collaborations." February 2007.

"The United States of Kubla Khan." first appeared in *MungBeing* magazine, Issue #7: "Fanaticism." April 2006.

"Vintage Scenes #2: 2010 Bernkasteler Lay Riesling Spätlese" first appeared in *MungBeing* magazine, Issue #55: "Spring." April 2014.

"The Last Session" first appeared as a chapbook for Dunhams Manor Press, an imprint of Dynatox Ministries, edited by Jordan Krall. February 2016.

"The Good Shepherdess" first appeared in *Zombies: Shambling Through the Ages*, edited by Steve Berman. Prime Books. Aug 2013.

"Remnants of Lost Empires" first appeared in *Starry Wisdom Library*, edited by Nate Pedersen. PS Publishing. December 2014.

"The Venus of Great Neck" first appeared in a Spanish translation in *Acronos II*, edited by Josué Ramos. Tyrannosaurus Books. June 2014. It appears here in English for the first time.

"Vintage Scenes #3: Morellino di Scansano, 2011 Vendemmia" first appeared in *MungBeing* magazine, Issue #56: "Reflections." June 2014.

"The Neurastheniac" first appeared in *Cassilda's Song*, edited by Joseph S. Pulver, Sr. Chaosium Inc. February 2015.

Contents

Unmentionable Treasures

A Few Words on the Work of Selena Chambers

In H.P. Lovecraft's "The Hound," a Decadent grave robber muses on his obsession with the beautiful and macabre—an obsession that spurs him and his partner to create their own nameless museum of plunder stolen from the dead, "unmentionable treasures" that "excite [their] jaded sensibilities." While reading through *Calls for Submission*, I was reminded of "The Hound"—the idea of gathering the lovely grotesque as a way of soothing the soul; of exploring aesthetics in a hope of achieving "respite from…devastating ennui." This collection of my friend Selena's writing, stories that are at once floral and severe, ornate but frugal, obscure yet accessible, would almost certainly have been given a place of honor had the nameless narrator and his companion found it buried beneath the black earth of a grave. They could not have found a better exemplar of their ideals.

I met Selena through a mutual friend while I was still living in Tallahassee. We were both aspiring writers still finding our sea legs when Selena and I workshopped a story of hers—a story that appears in a radically different form in this collection, "The Last Session." I have no memory of what I brought to the table that afternoon; what I remember is being intrigued by Selena's clarity of vision and understanding of what inspired her artistically. And I've been impressed, over the intervening years, how true she has stayed to herself.

This isn't to say Selena's artistic output has been one-note. In fact, Selena has achieved an amazing amount in many fields. Selena's short fiction masterpiece "The Neurastheniac" was recently nominated for a World Fantasy Award; she was nominated for a Hugo and a World Fantasy award for her work on the critically acclaimed *The Steampunk Bible*. To my great pleasure *Wandering Spirits*, her dazzling work of nonfiction that chronicles her adventures in Europe, following the footsteps of Victor Frankenstein, was recently collected and published in a pretty volume, the easier to luxuriously pore over. She was also an editor at online magazine *Strange Horizons*, and is currently editing a speculative fiction anthology called *Mechanical Animals*.

Selena's chops are manifest not only in her impressive bibliography. Her stories, which you are about to read, you lucky thing you, speak for themselves. On display in *Calls for Submission* is an artist unafraid to ride the stylistic merry-go-round, because her core is adamant. A Cthulhu-worshipping zombie Jeanne d'Arc stirs in her nightmare-wracked sleep beside a pile of crusty kids seeking out a legendary swimming hole; the lights that leak from a sinister Turkish puppet-show illuminate the grief-wracked madness of a couple the Great Gatsby himself would accuse of being self-absorbed. But all of these pastiches, cyphers, and tributes gel around unforgettable characters and genuine aesthetic intent.

Selena takes things seriously; it's one of the things I love most about her as a person, and also as a writer. Even when writing for one of the many, highly specific anthologies that appear every year in this new golden age of short fiction, she refuses to phone it in. Many of Selena's best stories have appeared in such— "The Neurastheniac" in Joseph S. Pulver's *Cassilda's Song*, "Dive In Me" in Beth K. Lewis' *The New Gothic*—and that is why I love her selection of a title so very much. There has been a bit of debate of late over whether writers of speculative fiction are being "overwhelmed" by anthology calls; whether there is a divide between those who write for a project, versus those who write because they were inspired sans prompt. Well, if there is such a divide, it is an artificial one. Artists have always worked for reasons other than the muse's clarion call. Bach and Mozart both composed for patrons; Caravaggio and Vermeer painted on commission. Arthur Conan Doyle came back to Holmes at the behest of his fans, and Lovecraft wrote to keep himself in beans. And yet, all of these artists managed to excel at their craft—and be subversive and avant-garde, as well.

I am inexpressibly glad Selena has felt called to submit her work—and inexpressibly glad she at times confides in me about her future artistic plans, desires, and goals. She inspires me and delights me every time we're together, whether on the phone, over social media, or too rarely in person. She also forces me to do better. Frankly, it's been difficult to write this introduction to Selena and her work, because all that needs to be said is that Selena is fucking awesome, and is an even better writer. Her work and her friendship keep at bay *my* devastating ennui, no grave robbing required. But, I'm lucky that way. Trust me, if all you ever get to encounter is her writing, you're still coming out on top.

—Molly Tanzer

Of Parallel and Parcel

"[Mrs. Poe] called me to her bedside...she took...a worn letter and showed it to her husband, he read it and weeping heavy tears gave it to me to read. It was a letter from Mr. Allan's wife after his death. It expressed a desire to see him, acknowledged that she alone had been the cause of his adopted Father's neglect."

—Letter from Louisa Shew to John Ingram, 28 March 1875.

I.

It rustled against my thigh under the dinner table. Pinned inside my shift skirt, my hands itched to touch it, to rip it apart. But I had to wait for darkness—for solitude—for my mother to go to sleep.

It was a letter from Richmond. Not from my cousin Eddy, as I had hoped, but addressed to him in a feminine scrawl that piqued within me a curious jealousy. I knew the letter was nothing to me. My thievery weighed on my conscience during dinner, and the only way to appease it was to feign ignorance of the day's mail.

"No letter from Eddy today?" I asked Muddy, my mother, as she sat down next to me at the table.

"God-a-mercy, Virginia, he hasn't even been out of Baltimore a week. He's probably too busy at the moment; probably hasn't even had time to unpack his pen."

"But he promised to write every day. Can he be so busy that he has to break promises?"

"We could have a letter by now, if he mailed from coach, but you know mail is sometimes lost. Be patient. We'll have two or three letters from Eddy, soon enough. Until then, we have a letter from Neilson to tide us over."

My cousin Neilson was a newspaperman and professional bore. He had recently married my sister Josephine, a paragon of feminine simplicity and illiteracy, and seemed to believe that through marriage I was his responsibility.

"Such a nice man. He has offered to take you in,

bring you up like a lady. Could be a good opportunity for you."

"To contract ennui."

"Nonsense. You can mature, be in society a bit before you marry. Then, if you still want to marry Eddy when you come of age, you can. If not—well, who knows, you might marry up in the world."

She dipped most of the potatoes on my plate, only a spoonful on hers. We had no meat, but there were still some beans Muddy had earned from sewing. She preached patience, but she was also desperate for Eddy's letters. They would contain money.

What little riches Eddy had, he shared with us. But it was not enough for him, let alone we three. Muddy was grateful for the attentions he paid us, but her gratitude waned when I gave him my hand.

Perhaps it was due to his father's erratic and mysterious behavior, which Muddy minced as "inconsiderate and foolish." Her brother David abandoned his consumptive wife and children in Virginia, and no one learned what became of him. Muddy would never say so, but I am certain she saw her brother's ghostly visage on my Eddy's face and worried he had also inherited his father's wanderlust.

And when she looked at my face, she saw her youth's shadow and worried it would fade into the same folds and wrinkles poverty bestowed on her.

When Eddy decided to regain his fortune where it was lost—in Richmond—she immediately solicited Neilson's help.

It's not that Eddy didn't try. He applied to teaching posts, but they came to nothing. The only steady income, as pithy as it was, came from his pen.

"If Neilson really wanted to help us, he would get Eddy a job at his newspaper."

"He is just being kind. You are too young."

"I'm almost thirteen! Eddy says that is an acceptable age in Richmond."

"Yes, but you are not in Richmond."

The letter scratched my skin through the cotton.

"Does he think I love Eddy against my will? Do you? I am more in possession of myself than Josephine, and she's twenty-three."

Muddy's fork clattered against the plate.

"It's not what you think it'll be. So you might want to consider going to Neilson's for a while. Let Eddy get on his feet; you finish growing."

I pouted over my potatoes: "Eddy will come back for us. He wants us with him. We are all he has."

"I know, child, but things can happen that change a man." The feminine inscription branded my flesh as Muddy spoke in-between her beans. "His prospects might change and we'll just be in the way. We need to look to your future."

II.

At bedtime, I snuggled next to Muddy. I planned to feign sleep until she fell into her own slumber; then, I would be alone with the letter. But the lugubrious womb of quilts and her embrace lulled me into dreaming.

I had two dreams, Louisa. The first was a calm and comfortable vignette. I sat in a bay window, watching Muddy stumble after a toddling boy—my son—through a garden. I was as old as Josephine, as old as I am now.

The boy walked up to the window and tried to hug me through the glass, squishing his chubby palms and forehead against the pane. Other mothers' hearts would have swelled with love. Mine shrank. I didn't even smile when Muddy sneaked behind him and scooped him up to shower him with kisses.

I had never seen my mother so happy. I should have laughed with them, but I was unmoved. I felt alone. There was nothing of Eddy in the child's face.

It was Neilson's doing, you see. Were I left in Neilson's care, he'd keep Eddy distant and marry me off to someone as respectable and tedious as himself.

Outside grew dark and Muddy grabbed her grandson and rushed into the house. The dream changed—no child, no landscaped garden—and you were there, Louisa. Even though I didn't know you then, you were there.

III.

The room is dark save the candlelit corner where a woman sits clinking a paintbrush against a water jorum. The flame casts unsettling shadows on her face: her eyelids smolder around orange embers. Eddy stands beside her at a window. I tell him that this stranger is a demon writing a receipt for my soul, but he is unmoved. The only thing that keeps me from crying out in fear are Muddy's calloused fingers sweeping across my scalp, braiding and entwining my hair. Each locket twists into the follicles. The hair-pins are cold and swim against my skin like iron eels.

"There, that looks quite becoming. Now, to make you a suitable collar." Her eyes dart around the room.

"Perhaps the sheet," the woman's voice reverber-ates throughout the floorboards. "You can drape it in folds around her neck."

"It's a fine linen. It will look as it ought. Eddy, come hold her."

Drafts have made his hands and clothes cold, as if each fiber held Boreas's bated love. He sits behind me, his hands sliding through my arms, encircling my waist, seeking warmth in my flat belly. He kisses my cheek as I lean into him. My husband!

"Virginia, you have to sit up. Eddy, make her sit up." He breaks the circle of warmth to stand by the bed. I am a rag doll in his grasp. My head hangs over my chest. My arms flounder like plucked wings. My sternum stabs at my lungs—.

White sheets are ruined by a whisper.

Muddy finishes primping me; Eddy lowers me onto the pillow. There is a rustling underneath the down loud enough to fill the room, yet I am the only one who hears.

Eddy spreads his coat over my legs and returns to the window. Muddy retreats to the corner to sew close to the light. Her eyes flicker between her stitches and my bed. Sometimes they wander to the strange woman and bulge at her paper and paints like they are rats.

"Must she paint Virginia now?"

Eddy stands over the woman, watching the swooping lines of my fleshy hue and shade fade into the pillowcase. He nods.

Muddy's eyes gleam across the room. "Oh, my child," she whispers, "You are too young."

He will not leave the portrait. I want to call to

him, but reclining makes everything gurgle. I strangle as a bloody brook bubbles in my throat. I begin convulsing, yet all I think about is the rustling echo from beneath my head. My fingers crawl under my pillow and find comfort at the crisp, dried texture of a dead fate.

It crackled like Muddy's snores.

IV.

I awoke thinking of the letter. In the window moonlight: Muddy's nostrils inflated and deflated. Alone, at last.

I tiptoed into the kitchen. The match roared over the wick. I covered the candle with my hand and listened for Muddy's undisturbed oscillations.

I unpinned the letter. The inscription glowed and expanded under the soft light. I wanted to tear it apart, but I softened the seal to look sun-warped.

The same feminine hand curled tightly over the paper. I read it, looking for betrayal and intrigue, but what I found was reconciliation.

You have not known us long enough to know Eddy was once a wealthy son. It is true he was orphaned, but his adopted father was a prosperous merchant who raised Eddy like his own. But Eddy was not the merchant's son. He was Poetry's son, and

Fortune disowned him.

A year before Eddy went to work in Richmond, he called on Mr. Allan, having heard he was ill. The new Mrs. Allan met Eddy at the door, and told him that her husband refused to receive him. The old man hadn't died yet, but Eddy came home with the only father he knew dead in his heart.

This letter from Richmond was from that same Mrs. Allan, now widowed. A confession: she had wronged Eddy. Mr. Allan had loved him—despite their differences—and died thinking of himself as Eddy's father. It was the widow who had instigated Eddy's neglect—for the sake of her children's fortune, of course. A year later, her Christian conscience nagged her and she invited Eddy back to his childhood home to return the remembrances Mr. Allan left him.

"If you do not come within the fortnight," it read, "I will assume you have refused me and will speak of it no more."

Here was a letter delivered by Fate.

Eddy had always felt his home was Richmond. He felt even more that he had been exiled, stripped of honor, orphaned again and again. These were the circumstances that brought Eddy to our home— that brought him to me. Familial ties were not the only thread that held us together. There was also a common sense of loneliness, of poverty, of being wronged. This widow's letter meant to rip Lachesis's stitches and return Eddy to the life he had known—he had loved—that I knew he yearned to regain through the undignified business of letters. But here, with or without toil, his adopted birthright could be regained. Returned to privilege, would he return to us, return to me?

Another raucous wave swelled out from the bedroom. It washed over me with echoes of dinner: "... things can happen that change a man. His prospects might change and we'll just be in the way. We need to look to your future." Recalling my twain dreams, I felt I had looked to my future enough.

And there you sit, Louisa—with your water jorum and smoldering eyes—painting me away—a strange demon no more.

I held the letter over the flame, but hesitated to let it burn for fear the smoke would wake Muddy.

I refolded Eddy's letter inside out—no longer addressed to anyone—and snuffed the wick, dissipating its faint extinguish with my hand.

I stumbled back to bed, laid the letter underneath my pillow, and smothered it until it was a dead fate.

The *Şehrazatın Diyoraması* Tour

The Constantinople street is drenched in pure sunlight, saturating almost all color from the scene. The tall, alabaster stone building that zigzags and narrows the passage casts a Payne's grey shadow onto the *ochre* cobblestones. Despite its disparity in hue, the street is made interesting by the people who populate it. In the background, children escorted by an old man are wrapped in tattered rags. In the midground, two women wearing blue and white *çarşafs* steady themselves to march past a female family of ill repute who catch the eye by leaving their marigold, emerald, and ruby silk brocade *entaris* uncovered.

The shrouded women also pass and ignore the dozen or so British tourists who stare at them wide-eyed and in awe. The concubines, however, leave the street and beckon these Westerners inside. It is with these women that the image transitions and the tourists who have been viewing this scene are escorted into the realm of Turkish delights without taking one actual step into the vice den.

Of course, they don't realize that. As far as they are concerned their bodies are being propelled. The tourists are so enthralled with the scenery around them they don't notice it is nothing but light streaming from the Şehrazat's orbs, and that they are standing and static around her in the diorama gallery of the Imperial Ottoman Museum.

The immersion begins the moment they enter the building.

Waifs hired from off the street usher them into an empty and barren gallery. The only artifact in the room is what appears to be a life-sized sculpture, but is, in fact, the main attraction: the *Şehrazatın Diyoraması*.

Dressed like a sheik's daughter with only her face and forearms exposed, she wears a beautiful variegated turban knotted at the side of her temple, and an aigrette of gold coins adorns her brow. She wears ribboned amulets and *pay-i-çifts* of pearls and turquoise, and underneath her kaftan flashes the violet embroidered, rose dusk silk of her *shalwar*. Her flesh is carved from ivory, and upon close inspection, was delicately put together with bronze ligaments and socketry. This allows for some movement—her head can swivel and her arms gesture and rest—but she is for the most part immobile. Her face is completely inanimate; her pulchritude is composed of general features—high cheekbones and full lips. She has solid glass eyes sans pupils and a face frozen in a pensive gaze. Special attention has been given to the earlobes, which are carefully carved and inlaid with bronze to better capture the gallery's acoustics. Sound is her only means of collecting information and receiving commands. Other than that, she does not mimic any of the other human senses.

She stands on a stage in the middle of the gallery with one arm extended to the door wherein enters her creator and master, Werner von Froeschner, a charismatic German scientist who before his renown as the Şehrazat's creator had gained repute for his achievements in Genevan Galvanism, von Kemplen mechanics, and advances in scaling down difference engines while optimizing their performance. Because he insists on being the only one who operates the machine, he has stayed in the capitol and become the master of ceremonies to the diorama tour.

"Ladies and Gentlemen, welcome to Constantinople!" Waifs circle the tourists with tea and biscuits. "I know you are all eager to begin our trek, but first

I want to introduce you to our guide.

"Now I know what you all must be thinking: here is just another Chess Player. But I assure you, this is no chess player. This…this is the future of—well, everything—but we get ahead of ourselves. But, today—for today—this is the future of travel, yes? How many times have you seen a Delacroix set outside of Constantinople and thought that you too would like to see that scene? Be a part of that exact scene? Ah, but you come to the Empire and you no longer see that exact scene." There are a few agreements among the audience. "We live in an Industrial world now. There is not much room left for Romance—no, my friends, I am afraid the visions of Gêrome and Delacroix are quickly becoming nothing but dusty relics hanging on an aristocrat's wall, and the experience you so longed for is ever fleeting… until now!

"You see, my friend Abdul Hamid is a traveler as well. He understands the romance that fuels such excursions, and as he visited my homeland he had his own vision—why not use all of this industry, all of this progress, to make a new thing of beauty? To make a new experience for the worldly traveler? To keep the East as it was without having to stay stuck in the past! His vision—the *Şehrazatın Diyoraması*!
"What you see before you is the marriage of art and science—the brainchild of some of the best minds in

both the East and West. He hired me to oversee the Şehrazat's design and construction. Osman Hamdi Bey, the Turkish painter who was one of the first here to embrace the French techniques and was so well acquainted with the style we needed, curated and created the synthesized images you will shortly see. Louis Majorelle, the French furniture maker who can often be found in a Constantinople café, was commissioned to design her body, but would you believe the Sultan himself—a great carpenter—constructed it!?" He pulls her flowing costume away from her abdomen to reveal the elaborate Marjorelle cabinet made of juniper wood inlaid with beech and ivory crocuses. Although it is shaped in the voluptuous style of a de Milo torso, its realism is blemished by two oblong doors inlaid with bronze knobs, which von Froeschner opens to reveal the contents within: a plethora of mechanical intestines that intertwine so densely, one cannot fathom what any of it is for.

Smiling at the quizzical expressions of those who gaze inside the cabinet, he closes her up. "You see, inside here is the *karanlık oda*—the darkroom—the camera obscura that projects this tour. This," he knocks on the torso, "this is the pride of the Ottoman Empire, for the diorama was devised and constructed by the Sultan's favored photographer, Bora Fahir Çağlar." He lets the skirts fall over the cabinet torso and walks behind the Şehrazat with a melancholic expression. "Sadly, he disappeared before he could see his genius realized. No doubt, he would have marveled at the illusion he helped create."

On that somber note, the waifs pull shut the black curtains. Someone from the audience exclaims: "Professor, you have evaded explaining how she works."

Von Froeschner wags a finger. "Yes I have. With all due respect, ladies and gentlemen, if I explained how this marvel works, I would destroy the illusion you came here to enjoy. We, here, are not interested in bragging about our scientific discoveries, although we easily could do so and change the world. No, we are here to provide you with an experience—so please, worry not on technicalities, just enjoy your holiday." He bends back down behind the Şehrazat, fumbling with her back as the room turns to pitch.

The tourists hold their breaths as a loud humming begins and exhale in delight as light composing the pale yellow and Prussian blue of Cappadocia shoots from her eyes and fills up the room. They forget about von Froeschner and the inner workings of the machine, and journey forth into the fantasies of poets and painters.

*　*　*

In the Turkish Bath, grossly modeled after the infamous Ingres image, ladies and gentlemen are witness to voluptuous women lounging, dining, wading, and ultimately having their decadent ablutions tended to by maids.

Most all of the audience respond in wonder at the scene, some a little abashed to be witnessing it in mixed company, but there is one—there is always one—who mutters: "But that maid there with the perfume. She isn't Moorish like the other maids in the scene." And before their eyes, the blonde maiden who had been powdering another's hair darkens. Other comments follow: "That eunuch's hair is too auburn and her skin still pale."

"Why don't they look us in the eye?"

"They seem too thin. Not voluptuous like the Venus."

And with every comment and observation, the image shifts, hair and skin brightens or fades, and the turbaned lute player who faced away from the tourists now boldly strums while staring them all in the eye.

These effects are so subtle and undisruptive that the tourists who speak out are unsettled at first that the machine seems to hear them, while simultaneously pleased that the machine obeys them. A group jester exclaims: "Perhaps there is a human brain tucked away in her bronze casted skull of hers, hey, von Froeschner?"

"If that were true," Von Froeschner retorts, "she'd still have human thoughts. Were that so, of what do you think they'd be?"

The rhetorical question sinks into the merry group who are quieted by awe as the projection exits the Bath and enters onto a bustling marketplace, crosses the street, and enters a café filled with dozens of young bearded men in turbans and fezzes huddled to discuss news of the day in a great vaulted marble establishment, its walls decorated with *iznik* tiles in the tulip fashion.

The shift is so seamless that the tourists are enthralled once again, and forget that with each critical utterance the projection changes into a more ideal vision—it is so imperceptible they forget they had even thought it, much less muttered it out loud. None of them consider that the image they see may be more romanticized now than it was before, and that the experience they are having is a false one. No, they came here to be comfortable. They especially disregard von Froeschner's retort and have no more notions of the dark rumors that were broached in jest.

*　*　*

Had von Froeschner equipped the Şehrazat with a voice box, she could have addressed the jester herself. She—he—may no longer be able to see or speak, but he can hear and think. He dreams what he can no longer experience. Sometimes, when he hears the tourists ask von Froeschner whether he—she—is "quite the storyteller like her mother, Scheherazade?" an allusion much encouraged by the scientist, he thinks his retort: *my mother died of consumption in Girit and told Christian stories to her older children while bedridden, and she named me Nikos Antonakis, not Bora Fahir Çağlar, not Şehrazat.*

But she cannot tell the tourists that Bora Fahir Çağlar was a deceit, and instead continues to project the falsehoods that most interest them.

The Sultan was interested in lies as well. They were a grand distraction from rumors, and the Ottoman Empire was becoming full of vile and horrid ones.

But behind every rumor is a semblance of truth. Nikos Antonakis learned this when he went to work as one of the myriad photographers called upon by the Sultan to document the Ottoman Empire with their lenses. Many of these photos became official tourist propaganda and souvenirs, but none of Nikos' images would be found in foreign scrapbooks; even less likely upon the gallery wall.

He began taking photographs that showed the classical grandeur and status of the Empire, but rumors of an uprising in his home village in Girit made him aim his lens beyond empirical glory and towards some unacknowledged Ottoman truths. He heard of other incidents and revolts in Armenia, and took his lens there.

The Photography Project had little tolerance for journalism, so Nikos sent his tintype testimonies to certain liberal reform newspapers under the Turkish name Bora Fahir Çağlar, thinking a proper Turkish name would give his work more credit. Even with the pseudonym, he knew he'd be found out and arrested.

So it was no surprise that, a fortnight after the photographs were published, police stormed his hut, beat him unconscious, burned down his darkroom, and carted him off to Constantinople to a dirty jail cell.

* * *

But he did not awaken in a jail. He found himself on a straw mattress shoved in the corner of a stonewall laboratory, his right foot chained to a ball. Standing over him was von Froeschner, wearing a reassuring smile and a lab coat splattered in oil. He spoke to Nikos in Turkish:

"You don't know me, my friend, but I know you. While it has earned you the Sultan's disfavor, I admire your work and have heard much about your methods. In fact, it is my admiration that has kept you alive; it can keep you alive if you will help me."

Nikos spat at his shoes. Von Froeschner nodded and gestured for the guards to unchain him.

"See, already you are freer than before. Please, let me show you something; it may change your mind." He motioned the guards to give Nikos over and led the photographer-prisoner over to a slab where lay the Şehrazat.

She was undressed, with her skull and cabinet torso open. Nikos could see how her appendages were attached via bronze-wired knitting. The inner workings that would confound the tourists when she was displayed were pulled away, and Nikos could see, deep inside her guts, three tiny gas lights sputtering cobalt flame, a slanted mirror that optimized and directed the lightening, and a spool on a rotating mechanism. Von Froeschner rummaged in the cabinet, connecting and attaching various things, and pointed to what Nikos would later learn was Bey's tableau scroll on an adjacent table.

"I think you know how to install that here." He watched Nikos place the scroll on the spool and came up behind him to ensure it was aligned. He closed her up, and walked to her skull. He gestured for Nikos to stand next to him. Nikos glimpsed the inside and saw that the skull housed a small brain connected to various internal prongs. The sight startled him, and von Froeschner placed a hand on his shoulder. "Ah, yes. It is disconcerting at first. It was generously donated to us from the Sultan, whose pet capuchin was ravaged by a tiger last week."

Where matter and metal met, blue sparks exploded when von Froeschner pulled a lever beside the slab. A soft hum emanated from her, and a bright light projected from her eyes to the ceiling, creating the pale yellow and Prussian blue of Cappadocia.

"There. You see?" Nikos marveled with mouth agape as the diorama became animated on the ceiling. The image was as clear and sharp as a photograph, but rendered in the palette of the Orientalists, making it the most realistic image he had ever seen. The image itself moved, not by rotation, but zoomed in and out of the scenery like binoculars. As amazing as that was, Nikos couldn't help but think: *it is inaccurate, like most paintings. It isn't real; it isn't truth.*

"What…what is this? A diorama?" he asked.

"Yes, for now she is a diorama, but she has the potential to become much more. The Sultan terms her a truth machine. People will believe what they see—it will be real to them. It will become memory—like a visceral dream."

"But it isn't true," Nikos muttered.

"The Truth is not real unless it can be seen—as you well know, a picture never lies."

Nikos stared up at the projection as it entered the Turkish Baths. "It depends on the picture. Many pictures lie."

Von Froeschner chuckled. "And there are many truths. There are harmful truths, just like there are beneficent lies. All are just means to an end."

"Whose end?"

"That is a good question." Von Froeschner turned off the machine and walked around the Şehrazat, running his hand down her cabinet torso. "We are learning that the brain's abilities are grossly underutilized. It is much like a difference engine, you know. It has electrical impulses that process and synthesize information at an uncanny rate, and yet we only use it for quotidian tasks, and it could be argued we barely use it for that. I want to test it—to challenge it. With constant stimulation, its capacity for performance could in theory increase exponentially, to eventually maintain a tintype-like memory that could store and recall information and perhaps eventually become clairvoyant based upon patterns and probabilities it perceives."

Nikos could not comprehend what von Froeschner blathered about, but he knew it was momentous, and the excitement of the new, of the truly revolutionary, welled inside him. It made him forget that he was a prisoner and why he had been imprisoned.

"All of that from the brain of a monkey?" Nikos looked away from the diorama to meet von Froeschner's lachrymose smile.

"Perhaps it could," he said. "But I am not speaking of this there." He pointed to the beating rose matter. "I am speaking of that here." He gently placed his finger on Nikos' temple. "This is what I need to help me."

Excitement soured into trepidation within Nikos. "Help you? I am just a photographer. What does this have to do with me?"

Von Froeschner nodded with a frown. "You are aware of the extreme disfavor you've garnered yourself? The Sultan wants your head, but he has no use for it other than to make it an example to others. But I have use for it, and so have asked him to give it to me. I admire your mind, you see? I want it to live—to share many truths."

Nikos looked von Froeschner in the eye. Von Froeschner nodded and then turned away. Before Nikos could ask von Froeschner his meaning, he felt a cold prick at the base of his head and entered an unknown darkness.

* * *

The café scene is now a distant one. The image pans over the hundred or so men sitting and dis-

cussing politics in traditional costume, and goes beyond the city passing the Basilica Cistern and flying
over the slate domes and white spires of Topkapı
Palace, soaring over the three courtyards until landing
on the Bosporus shore.

Underneath the current of the projections, Nikos
dreams of his homeland. Eventually, after being en-
cased within von Froeschner's contraption of charms
for several months, he was able to achieve what von
Froeschner had predicted, and under the constant
stimulation and processing of tourist information,
which included learning their languages, his mind
developed the ability to multitask, to dream and in-
habit his internal world of personal memory while
continuing to project the *faux monde* for the tourists, all while processing their cues to synthesize and
revamp the diorama.

The Bosporus sea reminds him of the shore where
he was born, and he thinks of his mother wasting
away.

He is distracted from the dream by the tourists'
gasps—not of the usual astonishment—but of dis-
taste and disappointment. The sea's flawless view is
obstructed by a consumptive Magdalene, who leans
over a bed of sand and seaweed and spews sputum
from behind her long stringy hair.

"Why, that woman is dying!" a matron proclaims,

and Nikos holds onto the image to make it clearer. The tourists see the shore disappear behind barren stone walls and several newly orphaned children tugging at their lost mother's soiled skirts.

Several of the female tourists wail at the pathos, upsetting their men.

"Von Froeschner!" a male tourist bellows. "This is grotesque. What is the meaning of this?"

Von Froeschner feigns ignorance and asks the audience to bear with what must be a glitch.

To their relief, they are lead out of the woeful house and into an image of a white stone church on the shore, the azul water lapping the pale yellow sand.

"Now that's more like it," says the bellowing Brit. Just then, the image becomes crowded with Turkish soldiers slicing *kilijs* into Cretan women and children; the church is engulfed in flames. The chiaroscuro haze is so realistic that the tourists panic, and some seek the doors. In response, the image leaves the Cretan massacre and enters the door of the church. The entire room darkens for a moment, and the complaining tourists quiet.

Slowly a stonewall laboratory fades into their vision, and once the image is fully developed they see von Froeschner standing in between two operating tables. On his right they can make out the Şehrazat, her head unbolted, brain exposed and blue sparking. It takes several moments for the exposure to reveal the other slab, but eventually the tourists make out the chiaroscuro depth of an open and empty human skull.

The tourists become frantic. The atramentous curtains are ripped from the rods, making the horrid image fade.

Those who haven't fainted or sought escape stare at von Froeschner and the orb-shining Şehrazat. The joke made fifteen minutes ago now hangs in the air like a noose.

Ignoring the tourists, who are demanding to be let out of the locked room, von Froeschner grins and saunters over to shut the Şehrazat down. She returns to her default position, her arm gesturing at the triumphant scientist musing over the mob scene unfolding before him.

* * *

The Constantinople street is drenched in pure sunlight, saturating almost all color from the scene. The tall, alabaster stone building that zigzags and narrows the passage casts a Payne's grey shadow onto the ochre cobblestones. Despite its disparity in hue, the street is made interesting by the people who populate it. Several dozen panting and pale Western tourists, sweating in their grey and pastel wools and cottons, faint and gesture wildly at shrouded women who ignore them, dazed by the seen and unseen of their dreams, bewildered by the scenes of Bora Fahir Çalğar and the truths of Nikos Antonakis.

Dr. Lambshead's Dark Room

About ten years ago, Dr. Lambshead published an article in the *Psychomesmeric Quarterly* about hypnotic techniques inherited from his grandfather, a great confidant of Herr Mesmer. Among Lambshead's mesmeric family legacy was the Valdemar method that enabled the doctor, so he claimed, "to extract from even the most cavernous subconscious those diseases that afflicted the soul, as demonstrated in the mesmeric stories of Edgar Allan Poe."

As a Poe scholar, the doctor's claims intrigued me and I wrote him requesting a demonstration. I knew the good Doctor could not resist a challenge, so to further intrigue him I mentioned that I felt riddled with a disease of influence that was affecting my work and love life, and offered myself up as the proverbial guinea pig. Within a fortnight I received an invitation to his house, "the only place," he wrote, "where the Valdemar method could be manifested."

Surprisingly, Dr. Lambshead appeared to have no maid or butler, and was already waiting at the door when I arrived. An ancient but spry man in a tailored silk bathrobe, he was headed down the hallway before I could put my bags down and greet him.

"To the matter at hand," he said. "Don't tell me a thing. That is for the Dark Room to show."

He waved me inside and led me to the back of the house where he pulled aside a faded Turkish rug to reveal a trap door that fell open into a dark and dusty staircase. He descended into that darkness, and I followed him down several flights, feeling my way around the rocky walls, until he suddenly halted and clapped his hands repeatedly. When he stopped clapping, several floating orbs illuminated the basement.

"Will-o-the-wisps," Lambshead said, "from the Iberian coast. I caught them with one of Nabokov's butterfly nets." I looked at the floating lights which graduated from green to purple, blue to red like childhood's LED sparklers. I held out my hand and one alighted on my finger—its touch cool as the Mediterranean.

"How…how do they…?"

"Float? Live? Glow?" He shrugged. "Curious, no?" This response disappointed me. It was unlike a man of science to pass up a chance to explain away the world. He smiled: "Even in this century, there are still wonders beyond explanation. They are rare, but they do exist, and it has been my hobby, I suppose you could say, to collect all the world's true curios, as you will see. But no more words for now unless prompted; it disrupts the process!"

We continued through the hallway, and the will-o-the-wisps grew brighter as we walked through the cabinet until we entered a dark chamber, empty but with the exception of two worn Louis XVI chairs.

"Ah, now we can really begin."

He sat in one chair and gestured for me to occupy the other. The will-o-the-wisps floated out of our hands and hovered between our eyes. They undulated, glowing and dimming in tune with my heartbeat that swooshed through my ears.

"I want you to watch the wisps," he whispered, "and tell me: have you experienced these following symptoms: soaring soul, existential exigency, speaking in cryptically symbolic metaphor, vertigo caused by sublimity, vision heightened by chiaroscuro, dead-dwelling, or head-swelling?"

"Yes," I said.

"To all?"

"Yes."

"Hmmmm…." His disbelieving expression ebbed into a dare-to-hope.

The two will-o-wisps glowed blindingly blue and I became dizzy and hot, and the doctor and the wisps became double exposed, and somehow I was split twain by the sides until there were two of me. One sat in front of Lambshead and the undulating wisps, while the other, conscious and seeing, was free to traverse the room.

"Do you suffer from daydreaming reflex with reveries that include blackbirds, scents of an unseen censor, or aberrant alliterative applications?"

Beady eyes glowed from the wisps, and wings fluttered by my ears. I smelled dried flowers and cut grass, upturned earth and the fading waft of fabric softener. I looked at my sitting-self in the chair and heard her indolent "Yes."

"What else do you see?"

The wisps left Lambshead and my sitting-self to illuminate the corners of the empty room where ebon bookcases grew from the walls and within them appeared objects that my sitting-self described:

Jaundiced blueprints of a non-Euclidian pendulum; a stuffed cat with a hissing throat encircled in white fur; a fractured skull chilling a broken bottle of blood-thick sherry; a tailor's mannequin wearing a white blood-soaked and dirt-streaked dressing gown, its neck a splintered pine plank engraved with claw marks.

Beside the cases stood a stuffed gorilla. I couldn't help but touch its fur, which turned to feathers and fluttered to the ground, revealing the tarred and malformed skeleton of a dwarf. Through its eye socket a gold beetle climbed out and over to a shelf that held a jar of putrescence and nestled itself in an open locket containing a strand of blonde hair speckled black.

At the very bottom of the bookshelves were several jorums filled with animated landscapes: tiny ships thrust between a maelstrom pint; a littoral liter with a weeping willow tree overlooking a craggy shore; and a quart of electrified clouds in the shape of women hovering over an abandoned manse, crying dust and leaves.

"What are these?" I asked Lambshead. From his chair he looked up to the ceiling, unsure of my voice's source.

"What do they look like?" he asked my sitting-self. I heard her describe the jorums and he smiled.

"Mood," he spoke into the ether, "They are jars of mood."

I squatted at the bookshelf and selected one containing the cosmos. Several minute stars swam like strawberry seeds within a phosphorescent jam. They churned and congealed into the sun heating the glass. It burned my hand and I dropped it. With a loud bang, it exploded on the floor, incinerating all within the jar and melting the glass, which pooled and cooled into a Bristol blue fetus.

Before I could retrieve it, I heard Lambshead command me awake and suddenly I was back in the chair—whole—and subject to his sherry-sweet breath. The bookshelves, the taxidermy, curios and jars were all gone, but on the ground remained the glass fetus, which the doctor rushed to rescue.

He coddled it in his palm. "This—this is what ails you!"

"A child?"

"Of the imagination, yes. You thought you had a disease of influence, but it is much, much worse. You have a disease of the *imagination*, probably from too much Poe. But don't worry, this here is your cure."

"I thought you said it was what ails me?"

"You are cured," he said, ignoring me. "And I have another child for my cabinet!" He waved the wisps away and they dimmed in rejection. Before I could ask what the other children were, he rushed me from the basement and out of his house.

I did not see where he kept the Dark Room's off-spring, and I suppose now I never will, but after I left Lambshead and his curious cabinet, I admit I felt a lot lighter. Before booting me off the steps, he gave me permission to write of my disease, which seemed to ameliorate my condition more.

Having been able to resume a normal life, I am forever indebted to that cabinet and to Dr. Lambshead. When I read of his death, just three years later, I mourned not only the loss of that great man, but also of his dark room and its soul-ware nursery that has inevitably become overexposed and returned to the ether.

Descartar

Remedios awoke to the bruja's smiling face. Arylola's wrinkles and teeth were brown and porous like a paper towel soaked in coffee grounds.

"It was that inquisitive Spaniard, no? The jellyfish man?"

Remedios sat-up on the couch and looked around the living room of a shotgun shack last decorated in 1979. The furniture was draped in copper and rust velour. The carpet was a shaggy avocado. It reminded her of her grandmother's house, except Abuelita would never have had a grass hut tiki bar where tequila, lemons, limes, and baskets of herbs mingled on the table with a blender. Was this standard bruja living? She had expected a dark and sulfurous hovel with furniture made out of cattle bones.

The normalcy unnerved her. Her presence at the normal abode unnerved her even more. She remembered going to meet Rollón at the bus station, her bags packed and her heart full. She waited for hours, watching the buses drive by. She didn't know which one carried her lover, but one thing was certain. . . .

"I was to go with him to Barcelona, but he left without me."

"I know. I found you on my way home from the market. You were on the side of the road in a puddle of vomit. I had to carry you here."

Seeing the old lady's thin limbs, it seemed remarkable she could lift her fruit basket, let alone a seventeen-year old girl. It was too much for Remedios, and she had nowhere to cry but in Arylola's arms.

"There, there, child. Let it out, let it out. He gets only one good cry, you hear? No man is worth a sea of sorrow. Especially that one. He wouldn't listen to a word I told him about those jellyfish. But then again, when have you last heard of a scientist listening to a curandera?"

Barcelona's Institut de Ciències del Mar had dispatched Rollón to sleepy Teconeuh to research rumors of a glowing jellyfish sighted by the fishermen, including Remedios's father. Rollón told Remedios that these "cnidarians," as he called them, had been sighted as far as Japan, and there were accounts of them from the British Isles, South America, and most of coastal Europe. Now, it seemed, their migration included the Gulf of Mexico. But the jellyfish were elusive, and the cream-skinned, pencil mustachioed biologist's studies turned toward Remedios.

During their affair, he never spoke of home, always deferring Remedios's inquiries to her own history. He loved hearing about her village childhood, which she divulged solely to keep his attention. Remedios was sick of her home the way native teenagers are. She wanted to hear of Barcelona, silk boutique dresses, walks down paved roads, street cafés, museums, opera—anything but fishing and village gossip. If Rollón did ever talk about himself, it was in context of the cnidarians.

Arylola tapped Remedios's shoulder, interrupting her reveries.

"But of course, you let him have you. Full moon or new moon? You can tell me. I birthed you and your sisters, after all. I'm practically a doctor."

Remedios hesitated.

They first made love under a full moon on the shore—a dusty plank of earth falling off into wet darkness. A wave would rise and vie for a moonbeam, then fade back into nothing. Rollón's silvery skin ebbed against her bronzed flesh, their moans drowned by waves and wind.

"All the moons, I guess." Remedios muttered.

"And when did you last have your menses?"

"I. . .I don't know."

Arylola patted her arm. "It is what I thought: he has not completely left you."

"What does that mean? I'm pregnant?"

"Oh, yes. When you get as old as me, you can pick them out of a line up. I knew it when I found you."

"No. That can't be."

"I'm sure it can't, but it is," Arylola sighed. "Don't bore me with a list of contraceptives you may or may not have used. I've heard it all, seen it all. Despite how unique and terrible you think your situation is, you are not the first to be forgotten. Perhaps he has a wife or a snobby mother who would have fainted at the sight of your dark skin. But what does it matter? He's gone, and *you* are knocked-up."

"You don't know? You're supposed to know ev-everythi—." Arylola's pruned hand clamped Remedios's mouth.

"What will knowing do for your situation? Give you comfort? That will last as long as your next bout of morning sickness. No, child. I've seen it all before. I've known women who drowned their children after falling in love with a new man. What do you think *he* did? Disappeared, just like your jellyfish man.

"Compared to them, your situation is ideal. There's hope for you. My advice: forget him and think of the child."

Remedios swiped Arylola's hand away. Think of the child? Remedios only thought of the embarrassment and shame. She'd left her family a note explaining her elopement, and now she would not only return jilted, but carrying another hungry mouth.

"I can't! I can't have a baby. What will people say? My father will kill me."

"Perhaps you should have thought of that before you made love under the full moon. But do any of them think? No, just love until it's too late."

Remedios struggled to not weep again as she recalled her last night with Rollón. They sat on the shore, arm and arm.

"The Institute is growing impatient," he stared at the tide. "They want me home."

Remedios wondered if he was sullen for her or his failed expedition? She gazed at the ocean and wished for the glowing jellyfish to appear. Then he would stay. But the dark ocean remained.

"You don't have to return home empty-handed," she said.

Rollón considered her.

"You would abandon everything for me?" His fingers brushed her face. "That's worth all the glowing jellyfish in the sea." He cupped her chin and pulled her towards him.

In his kiss, Remedios felt he meant it. He had meant it, yet he had abandoned her.

"If only those damn fish had appeared. Rollón was right, it was just a fisherman's tale. But father said he saw them; father never lies."

"That's right. Your father never lies, and neither do I. There are jellyfish, all right. Don't believe me? Go to the beach tonight. I guarantee you'll see them."

"Why tonight and not any of the countless nights Rollón and I looked for them?"

"Because there was no reason for you to see them. Tonight—if you choose—you will."

There was a change in the old woman's mood.

Arylola slowly stood up from the couch and walked over to the herbal tiki bar. Remedios expected her to begin tearing into the leaves, grinding them with a pestle and mortar. Instead, Arylola arthritically bent over a refrigerator nestled by the bar and pulled out a can of pineapple juice and a brown paper envelope. Small, unlabeled, brown bottles lined the refrigerator door. Arylola's gnarled fingers played over them before she snatched four bottles and slammed the door shut. She poured the juice and ice into a blender and turned it on. A bobble-head hula girl swayed with the white noise.

"The pineapple is nature's blade. The vitamin C will shave anything clinging inside you—cut it loose." She began pouring from the brown bottles. "We have Blue Cahoosh to make the uterus contract, and a little bit of Black Cahoosh to soothe the cervix. This stuff is extract of tansy flower. This'll make you bleed like Mary." She fumbled with the envelope and poured in yellow dust. "Therefore, you need yeast. Lots of vitamin B. Makes the blood and energy strong. And a dash of Pennyroyal to send it home. Lucky you, it's last of the batch."

The blades whirled and transmuted the healthy yellow of the juice into sluggish grey sand. It clumped into the cup. Arylola pulled from behind the bar and stuck into the sludge a red straw and matching miniature umbrella.

"Now, you know the ingredients, but do you understand what this is? This is a glass of crushed pain. Before you drink this, you need to think really hard whether you want to get rid of your little Spaniard. Like the father, you can't have him back."

Remedios's throat contracted. She understood she was dumped, but the ever-awning question of Rollón's blatant deception confused her.

"But Rollón meant it!"

"They all mean it until they change their mind."

Arylola's blunt wisdom swirled and bubbled in Remedios's brain until the simple truth surfaced: Rollón had changed his mind.

Remedios eyed the sludge. She wanted to be rid of him completely. "I. . .I will repay you."

The old lady shook her head and placed the sweating glass in Remedios's hand.

It smelled like crushed cockroaches, but Remedios took out the umbrella and straw and choked it down while the old lady watched.

"Every drop. It will take an hour or so to work. Go wait at the beach. No one will see you when it hits."

"You're not coming with me?"

"What could I do? It's out of my hands now. Your decision; your consequences."

Remedios fought against the citrus spume oscillating in her stomach.

"Arylola? How. . .how much will it hurt?"

"You just drank a poison cocktail! You'll be lucky it doesn't kill you. What do you think I am, magic? Presto, now you see the fetus, now you don't?" Then she grew quiet, her mind swimming away. "All those children," she mumbled to herself. "All those poor bastards."

"What about the jellyfish?"

Arylola's eyes refocused. "They'll be there, you'll see."

* * *

Cirrus clouds veiled and unveiled the full moon. The water lapped Remedios's feet and the wind sandblasted her cheeks. A slight pang began to throb in her abdomen, and with each pulse she became convinced she had been wronged, punished for having loved and wanting more than her village could give. She cursed the village. She cursed God. Most of all, she cursed Rollón.

Had the jellyfish appeared and Rollón stayed, how would he react to this news? Would he take her in his arms and rhapsodize their future?

Remedios looked at the choppy sea and knew that she would be seeing the same scene after all.

The wind picked-up, and Remedios thought she heard weeping in its breath. Lights flickered at the bottom of her eyes. She looked down at the sea and saw floating on the surface hundreds of little golden lights, bobbing and floating like phosphorescent sea grapes.

The glowing jellyfish! They had come like Arylola said.

Remedios waded into the water to look closer. She

stood waist high in the churning sea. Around her, ten-foot waves ebbed into twenty-foot waves until they grew as tall as any Barcelonan skyscraper. One such wave ascended and towered over her.

The clouds unveiled the moon, transforming the standing, rushing water into a specular surface in which Remedios not only saw herself, stricken and wan, but hundreds of women flailing their arms in weeping pantomimes behind her. Remedios looked back but saw only blowing sand.

Then the cries stopped. When she looked in the wave again, the women were gone.

The wave crashed upon her and dragged her deep underwater, flooding her nose and mouth with salt water.

Remedios opened her eyes in the burning brine. The bright legion above illuminated what swam below. The glowing bulbs were egg-shaped translucent films wrapped around two or three white heat filaments attached to fleshy tubes. These tubes were anchored several fathoms underwater to translucent jellyfish bells containing infants no younger than six weeks, toddlers no older than five years. Their eyes and lips were shut in plastic slumber like baby dolls.

Remedios's abdomen contracted and warm blood jetted between her legs, scaring the fish that swam amongst the floating wombs. The blood disturbed the cnidarians, and their molded lids peeled and glared with gelatinous, black eyeballs. There was a whimper, a quiver of cherubic lips, before they all yawned gargled sobs that bubbled inside their sacks.

Remedios stroked and kicked away from the crying things, fighting against currents and cramps. Back on land, she gasped for air and collapsed on the sand.

How many were there? Hundreds, thousands—an entire sea of unwanted children by lovelorn women like her.

Remedios felt the shame Arylola tried to conjure in her. She stuck her fingers down her throat to make herself vomit, but most of the poison had been digested. Only dry heaves, sand, and an acidic, grassy aftertaste yielded. Like the father, she could not get the child back.

The infants' cries continued to swirl in her ears. She wanted to run, but her paroxysms kept her paralyzed in a crab-like crouch. Deep within her womb, it felt like thousands of tentacles were whipping her lower intestines, nematocysts were shooting into her ovaries, slashing her fallopian tubes. The blood flow grew thicker; leach-like clots crawled out of her soaked panties and down her thighs.

With each crashing wave, the glowing jellyfish swam closer to shore.

Remedios grunted against the red pain, until she felt something pass through her. In-between her legs glowed a plankton-sized cnidarian, its tentacle zig-zagging in the wet sand until it found water. Exhausted, she curled on her side and watched the tiny jellyfish swim to its flickering family.

Her eyes grew heavy. She wanted sleep. Perhaps when she awoke, she would be somewhere new. She no longer cared if it was in Barcelona with Rollón, just somewhere far away.

One by one, the lights disappeared underwater. Only an infinitesimal beam remained, burning until Remedios went away. Then it bobbed and joined the others.

Vintage Scenes #1

Bandol, Château La Rouvière, 2002

In the storefront of Nice's oldest cave, myriad dusty bottles line the oak-paneled walls and tumble out of decorative wine casks. Among them loiters three tourists: an older couple that are Australian restaurateurs and a young American girl of seven and twenty. While the couple dismisses the entire stock with blasé eyes, the girl discusses a purchase with Théophile, the resident sommelier.

"Are you going to take it home?" he asks her.

"No. I want to drink it before then. Maybe I should just get the cheaper one, although I loved what we tasted. What was that again?"

Théophile explains how the Bandol vintages work:

the youngest one could ever get would be three years old—when Bandol was ready to drink—but its best attributes really appeared after five years, and were perfect by ten.

"But the oldest we have right now is the '02, which you tasted." He hands her the bottle, and her gaze flickers between it and its price posted on the display.

"Can I see the new bottle?"

As she considers the two Bandols, the Australians leave, mumbling over their shoulders "Thanks" and "Much obliged." The girl waves after them, but as soon as the door closes, she scowls at Théophile.

"If only we all aged as well as this Bandol." Théophile does not understand her until she adds: "I really liked what you said to them."

"Because?"

She shrugs and casts her gaze back to the bottle.

The tourists had come to the cave to sample the best of the *vins de Provence* in the oldest cellar in the region. The girl had come first, and late, even by French standards, and Théophile refused to give a tasting to only one person, but then the Australians arrived and argued that they were on time. It had been a slow day with barely any sales and 45 euros was not a bad way to round off the till, he realized.

So, Théophile took them down to the cellar and poured them each a glass as they settled in across from him at the table.

It was all routine—the sniffing, the swirling, the swishing—with the Australians throwing out bouquet and palate terms to show that they were already aficionados. The girl seemed timid—she blushed every time she spoke French, which was not often now the Australians were there—and she sipped quietly. It was all proceeding quickly, until Théophile's attempt to cross his knee knocked the table, propelling the cork down to the Australian husband's hand.

"Don't have much use for these, anymore." He picked-up and inspected the cork.

Théophile ignored him to focus on finishing the tasting, but was surprised when the girl spoke: "What do you mean?"

"They're things of the past. You don't see them much anymore. Screwcaps are the way now."

"Oh, yes. There is still debate about that in the States."

"Well, it is just simple economics. When I order wine for my restaurant, I want the guarantee that it'll all retain its value. Almost every wine I buy is screwcap, and the spoilage has been reduced 100 percent. I used to pour out eighteen bottles a night;

now, I sell every one."

"Plus it is bad for the environment, you know," his wife added.

"But aren't the new corks plastic?" said the girl.

"But think of the rainforest!" retorted the wife.

"And the trash heaps! Besides," said the girl. "Aren't screwcaps only a short-term solution? Don't they get brittle after a few years?"

The Australian husband guffawed. "It's a long enough solution to keep my inventory rotating."

The girl looked at Théophile who stared and rotated his glass in a meditative effort to ignore the old man.

"Is there much debate in France?" she asked. Théophile cut his eyes at her and sipped from the Bandol. He hated this conversation, but he was never a man to turn down a shot at the soapbox—something his boss criticized him for quite often because you cannot stand on a soapbox without breaking a few bottles, costly ones at that.

"For me, it is blasphemy. That is not the tradition." He poured more Bandol in his glass, and held the bottle up. "It is not the same without the cork. The smell, the taste, the sound…." He mimed unscrewing a cap from the bottle. "It changes the whole ritual that raised me. The whole point—the experience—is ruined. For one bottle to be spoiled on occasion makes the enjoyment more precious. It is my life you speak of in terms of spoilage. No, I do not recognize this." His manner was vehement, and he folded his arms and stared over everyone as they silently finished off their wine.

With such a poetic outburst, Théophile expected to sell nothing, and was surprised when the American girl wanted to buy—the expensive bottle no less.

However, the longer she considers the young and aged bottles, the more Théophile doubts her sincerity until she finally answers his question:

"You made me realize something. Drinking wine dismisses the future. Sure, you bottle it and wait for time to go buy until it is ready to drink, but when the cork pops, the best parts of the past are released and realized again."

"Oh?"

"Eight years. Just think of the life lived between bottling and uncorking. What were you doing when this was bottled?" She gestures with the '02, then the '07. "And this one?"

The synesthetic surge of the past makes Théophile forget about the sale.

"I left Toulon to work at the château, making barrels and rolling them to the house from the winery.

And then I left Bandol to come work here."

"So this really has been your life?" He nods.

"Eight years ago, I'd never left home, and I'm pretty sure I didn't know Nice existed much less Bandol."

"But now you are here for...?"

"Another week."

"And you've been here how long?"

"Three weeks."

"A month on the Côte d'Azur! A rare trip. You will be leaving just as everyone arrives. It is just as well, it is hell here when tourist season starts."

"*When* it starts?" the girl laughs and hands him back the *jeune bouteille*. "You've convinced me. I think I want to enjoy this one and go back to 2002 for a while."

For the first time that day, the sommelier smiles, and gives the girl a generous discount.

Dive in Me

with Jesse Bullington

The girls were a gang of three: a triad, a triumvirate, or what have you. Like the Gorgons and Moirai before them, they never made a move or decision separately. So when Spring was missing from their usual hook-up spot in the kudzu-veiled lot behind the Hoggly Woggly one Saturday morning, the gang was thrown into a state of chaos.

"Where the fuck is she?"

"You don't think she got busted last night, do you?"

Gina paused to consider this, because it was a real possibility. They had been in the alley behind the skating rink throwing bricks at streetlights until the girls were broken up by crescendoing sirens and red and blue illuminations. In such desperate if not rare instances, they would all separate and regroup later.

"Nah, if she got bagged, we'd hear about it right?" Gina sat on a vine-cushioned log.

"Um, how?"

Gina pointed at the nearby pay phone. "You get a phone call, don't you?"

"Uh, yeah, to call someone that can bail you out. She knows we can't bail a dog out of the pound, much less her skanky bitch ass from jail." Moira seemed pleased with this comparison and either ignored or didn't notice Gina's growing concern. Bullshitting nosy cops was one thing, and actually running from them not unheard of, but so far none of them had actually been caught.

"Okay, well, she'd call her house, then," said Gina. "If she's not home, Hughes'll know where she's at."

Gina dug in the cavernous pockets of her baggy jeans for a quarter as she picked up the pay phone with her other hand, so she didn't see what was coating it until her fingers closed on cold, slimy slickness. She yelped and pulled her hand back, quickly looking around to make sure Moira hadn't seen her chickenshit reaction before she took a better look at the nastiness tangled around the phone. The parking lot and pumps were mostly empty, and, turning her attention back to the now-dangling receiver, she saw dripping duckweed wrapped all around the black plastic phone. Wiping her hand on her jeans, Gina smiled—that wasn't a bad gag, winding some shit around a phone. She would've used poison ivy, personally, and limited its use to the earpiece. That wouldn't provoke the same immediate revulsion, but whatever dumbass picked it up would grind the ivy into their ear before they noticed what was up. Tearing off the duckweed, she rang Spring's house.

"Yeah?" Hughes sounded groggy. It was, after all, noon o' clock, so Gina had either woke him up or caught him in the middle of his morning burn. He was Spring's boyfriend, and was a lot older than the girls. He claimed to be sixteen, but Moira suspected he was really twenty-one, because he always had booze and, more favorably, weed. She could picture him in a shredded Pearl Jam shirt and Superman boxers, his stringy red hair screening his bloodshot eyes.

"Hughes! Where the fuck is Spring? She was supposed to meet us behind Hoggy Wogs."

"I dunno…she was supposed to be crashing at your house."

"No, she wasn't," said Gina. Moira motioned at her that she was going inside to get a soda.

"Look, she told me she was sleeping over with you lezzers, and y'all were hitting the sinks today. That's all I know. Now fuck off." The line went dead.

Gina walked into the store to find Moira flipping through an issue of *CREEM*.

"What'd he say?" she asked without looking up.

"God," said Gina. "He's so fucking gross."

"Oh, I dunno. I think he's cute. Kind of has a Layne Staley thing going, you know?" Moira turned the magazine around to show Gina an Alice in Chains spread to prove her case.

"I'm sure he'd cream himself to hear that, Moira." Moira frogged Gina in the arm. "Jesus, ow! Well, whatever, according to his stoned ass, Spring never came home last night, and is supposed to be hitting the sinks with us today."

"We didn't talk about swimming."

"You think there was some mix-up, and she's waiting for us at one of the holes?"

"Could be. I guess we could check out the usual suspects, if your brother will pick us up."

"Fine. I'll go call him."

Gina had just dropped her last quarter in the phone when a long, distended shadow fell over the wall in front of her.

"Damn, but that is one sorry lookin' bitch!" The familiar voice was right behind Gina, making her jump. "Don't tell me your pimp lets you out of the crack house looking like that."

"Where've you been?" asked Gina, trying not to let her relief show as she wiped her sweaty bangs from her forehead and turned to Spring. "We've been looking all over, and Hughes said—"

"Suicide Sinks. It took all night, but I found those bitches!" Spring offered up the jagged grin of a girl who had never been to the dentist and was in general a hot fucking mess. She was covered in sweat, XXL flannel and parachute jeans not being the breeziest summertime attire. Her fading Kool-Aid dye job shed splotches of color on her shoulders and the parking lot.

All the relief Gina felt at finding Spring curdled in her stomach. When the other two had talked about finding the fabled sinkholes, she had gone along with it, because of course she had, but the possibility of the place really existing, much less their discovering its location, had never seriously darkened her imagination.

"Who were you calling?" asked Spring.

"Dave." When Spring wrinkled her nose, Gina said, "He sucks, but he'll drive us anywhere we wanna go, so long as Moira's with us. Unless Prince Charming in Chains got his license un-suspended?"

"Don't matter," said Spring. "We're walking—this is top secret, for skanks' eyes only."

"Oh."

"Moira inside?" Gina nodded. "You got any smokes?"

Gina nodded again. "Yeah, I lifted some Dorals from my stepdad, but they have to last all weekend. See if you can lift a pack from inside, or Hey Mister that redneck."

"That dude looks like a bitch—what kinda self-respecting good old boy drives a Kia? I'll try my luck in the pigsty, and get Moira to buy some jerky. It's a long walk to the Sinks from here; I've been running back here all fucking morning. And you Hey Mister that pussy anyway, you can't have too many coffin nails, Gina, not before Suicide."

Gina eyed Spring's damp hair and clothes. Nobody knew where Suicide Sinks were, if they even existed, and all of the usual swimmable sinkholes were at least a twenty-minute drive away—no way Spring was running that route. Gina also wondered if it wasn't just sweat from the balls-hot morning. "Did you...You went swimming there last night?"

"I wouldn't dive in without you and Moira! We're all going in together."

Great, Gina thought. Then Spring was gone, her

heavy jeans swishing as she darted into the store. Gina looked forlornly after her. It wasn't even noon yet and was hotter than hell, the leaves of the kudzu on the gas station wall dripping in the still, muggy air. Walking anywhere in this heat sounded retarded, and the promise of a swim at the end actually made it worse, for a change.

* * *

Anything that makes you feel alive can't be all that bad. This was the mantra that Gina used to justify all sorts of dubious adventures with Moira and Spring, the other two being decidedly less cautious than she when it came to, well, everything. Gina was the brains, and the other two were the balls not that she would ever voice such a sentiment, since they were also both a lot punchier than her. This plot, however, didn't give her the same queasy-awesome thrill as smashing streetlights or boosting shitty jewelry from Claire's, though the threat of police or pissed-off parents was a lot smaller. This plan filled her with dread. For the first hour, she smoked cig after cig, trying to come up with a plan on how to either talk them out of it or get herself out of it. She was just waiting for an opening, but Moira's enthusiasm kept common sense out of the conversation as they followed Spring until the cracked sidewalks gave way to the long grass that bordered the old highway leading out of town.

"C'mon," Moira said. "Tell us!"

"Fine," Spring said. "But it's nothing major. Just don't tell Hughes, you know how he gets."

Moira gave Gina a meaningful look. *How he gets?*

"When you bitches dipped out on me, I barely got away from the cops. Some Woodvillians were leaving the skate rink, and I bummed a lift with them. Couple of dirtbags and this spooky fat girl. They were going to hop a fence at some motel and go swimming, but, halfway there, Thick Girl mumbled something about Suicide Sinks. These goons knew where it was, and, even though they gave me a hard time, I talked 'em into taking me out there instead of hitting the motel pool. Those dirtbags took me right to it!"

"How do you know it was really Suicide?" said Moira. "And not some random redneck mud puddle?"

"I could feel it, right? Like, a sick sense."

"Sixth," said Gina. "Sixth sense."

"Sick Sense sounds better," said Moira. "That'd be a cool band name."

Typical stupid Florida woods bordered the half-dead highway out there, with rotten old shotgun shacks set back in the pines. The houses were mostly abandoned, and what little traffic passed them on the road consisted of semis and company trucks for the chemical plant. At last, they reached a particular overgrown dirt road that looked the same as every other turnoff they'd passed—barred by barbwire and flanked by flapping *No Trespassing* signs stapled to trees. Spring glanced up and down the highway and, seeing the coast was clear, ducked under the wire and booked it down the grassy track. This was a familiar ritual, and Gina and Moira were right behind her, the triad not slowing until they were well out of sight of the highway, their clothes instantly sopping from the sprint.

"I heard Hawk Point was condemned," said Gina once she'd caught her breath enough to light a cigarette. Talking about stuff with her friends always made it less creepy, more laughable.

"Huh?" Moira found a stick to break in half and toss back into the woods.

"I think this area was called Hawk Point," said Gina.

"Sounds like an ancient Indian burial ground," said Moira, then added. "Ba-chawk!"

"Shut up," said Spring and Gina simultaneously. Gina was secretly relieved to have Spring on her side. Usually she and Moira made a constant racket, even—especially—when they were doing something furtive.

"Hawk Point was one of the first suburbs this far out of town," said Gina. "Quiet place to raise a family, good property values, and not too close to all the rednecks and *black people*." This last she said in a hushed, scared old-white-lady voice. "But then something happened."

"Dun dun *dunh*!" said Moira.

"You guys know how sinkholes—how they'll just…" Gina gulped, the air thick in her throat. "*Devour* whatever they open up under. A whole house, yard and all, isn't unheard of."

"No shit," said Moira, snatching Gina's cigarette from where it languished between her fingers. "So?"

Gina scowled at Moira. "So, the fact is a sinkhole opened under *every* house in Hawk Point, every single one. *At the same time.* Middle of the night, when everyone was at home in bed, the ground just…swallowed them up. Houses, cars, playgrounds. *Dog* houses. Nobody got out. Geologically speaking, the incident was a phenomenon."

The only sound was the girls' jeans scratching against the grass that sprouted in the middle of the road and the droning of insects, and then Moira said, "I call bullshit, dude. No way a bunch of picket fencers got sucked into sinks without everybody in town knowing about it."

"This was years and years ago," said Gina. "And everyone *does* know about it. You saw the signs—'No Trespassing'—the ground's unstable."

The dirt track they were walking joined a narrow paved road, but one so ancient the ragged blacktop was mostly hidden under countless generations of rotting vegetation.

"The whole place is fucked, and not just because of the sinks," Gina continued as they veered onto this new path. "Before they got sunk, those entitled motherfuckers who lived here were so lazy that they poured oil and all their trash into the river rather than drive to the dump."

"Yeah," Spring said. "I asked Ms. Hannah about it. She said it was because it was close to the river and caverns that the ground was probably already eroded and too soft, or whatever, and the developers fucked it up with, uh, putting in a sewer thing or something."

"Ha-ha, yeah, they pissed Earth off and she opened up and ate them all!" Moira goosed Spring, and snatched her hand back. "Damn, dude, you're freezing! You sure you're not sick, fever-dreamed all this shit up?"

Gina looked at the sweat beading off of Spring's flushed face. She didn't *look* sick, and they were all pretty sweaty. A raptor soared overhead and landed in a pine tree.

"I'd kill to be freezing right about now," Spring said. "You must've been nipping from Hughes's stash again, Moira, or maybe you got frostbite from fingering Gina's frigid snatch."

"Bleh! Anywho, I bet that shit is nasty," said Moira. "The sinks, I mean, not your 'gina, Gina. I'm sure you're a very clean girl. Spotless, even." Gina ignored them and took interest in the sky. Moira continued: "You'd think they'd have put up some other warning signs, or something."

"Uh, you mean like all the signs we passed?" Spring shook her head, then dramatically swept her arm to the side. "Or that one over there?"

"No fucking way," Moira whispered. Then, substantially louder: "No fucking way!"

The ornamental boulder wore a mantle of kudzu vines, the thickly etched letters on its face outlined in moss. At its base, shredded warning signs mixed with the dead leaves like offerings at an altar. Moira did a victory pogo while Spring smugly watched Gina. *Hawk Point*, it read.

Beyond the sign was a much more serious barricade than the wire they had ducked back on the highway, but the galvanized gate was built to keep out cars, not juvenile delinquents on foot. As soon as she landed on the age-warped blacktop on the far side of the gate, Gina felt her stomach twist up, like she was getting cramps. It seemed louder on this side, the bug noises echoing through the hollows, Moira's braying voice ricocheting off the pines.

"Whatever happened out here, they were fucking with sacred ground," said Gina, and almost meant it. Remembering Moira's crack from before, she said. "Ain't there Miccosukee burial mounds around here? Maybe we shouldn't be fucking around here either."

"Maybe you shouldn't be such a puss," Moira said, sticking her tongue between her fingers in retort to the bird Gina was shooting her.

"It doesn't look that bad," Spring said once Moira and Gina had settled down. "You'll see."

They marched on. Spring retrieved a fallen branch to bat down the sticky banana spider webs that frequently blocked their path, and Moira scoured the ground for pine cones to kick. Gina continued to smoke and ruminate. As if Hawk Point's history wasn't disturbing enough, there was the reason everyone called this place Suicide Sinks. It wasn't that people came here when they were Kurt-minded, but just that every once in a while, some kid would go missing, and, after several weeks of searching, they'd find him floating down the river thirty miles from anywhere he was supposed to be. Reports on these dumbasses would show they hadn't been murdered or messed with, just drowned somehow, and eventually they figured out with maps or sonar or something that they all must have tried to dive the Suicide Sinks and failed. Like a lot of sinks, these were supposed to be connected by underwater caves.

And of course there were plenty of kids who never showed up in the river, or anywhere, period. Gina couldn't stop imagining herself swimming into some bloated corpse's arms and being drowned in its empty embrace…until the image became her and Moira and Spring floating lifelessly among all the other divers over waterlogged houses.

"Listen," Gina said. "I don't think I can dive with you, Spring."

"Why?" Spring asked.

"I suck at diving, man. I can't hold my breath for shit, and we've been doing all this walking and smoking and…" She hesitated. "And if you two dumbasses get in a jam, I can go for help."

Moira began to splutter, but Spring held up her cigarette to Moira's mouth. "Put a butt in it, Moira." Moira took the cig and puffed, winking at Gina through exhaled smoke.

Spring stared at Gina for awhile as they all continued walking.

"You don't think we can handle it?" Spring's voice was odd. Gina couldn't tell if she was concerned or contemptible of the assumed doubt or what.

"I know you can hold your breath forever. You I'm not worried about—" Gina darted her eyes at Moira. "Moira probably could too. It's just you don't know what's down there. No one does. Anyone who's ever dived there has never come back. That doesn't concern you?"

"Pfth. Tons of people do it. Those dumbasses from last night did it right in front of me, no problem. Anyone who doesn't come back drowns because they were either too fucked up, or just bullshit swimmers."

"What about that one dude," asked Moira. "The pro diver, or whatever, they found in the river last summer?"

Spring cut Moira a hellish look, and Moira just shrugged and lit another smoke with the dying ember of the previous butt.

"He was probably bullshit, too. I am not bullshit, and I'm not afraid to dive."

For the first time in their friendship, Spring seemed upset. Tears welled in her eyes. The intensity on her friend's face made Gina uncomfortable. She knew swimming was Spring's thing—everyone had a thing: Gina rocked math and the drums, and Moira was awesome at reconstructing clothes and doing hair. Spring *was* a killer swimmer, and a diver, too, but this...this emotion, this fear on Spring's face, was totally out of character, and it creeped Gina out. She had a notion, a fluttery feeling in her gut, that not just diving, but *surviving*, Suicide Sinks was so important to Spring that nothing, not a damn thing, could talk her out of it now. Their march had already gone too far to be deterred, and now Moira and Gina's fates were tied into these stupid sinkholes, also.

The girls stopped walking, and the heaviness of the heat and the insect thrumming of the forest weighed down on them, palpable, relentless. Gina sighed it off and began to air guitar the opening bass riff to Nirvana's "Dive."

Moira giggled and put her arm around Spring as she began to sing an altered version of the chorus: "Dive! Dive! Dive! Dive with me!"

Gina joined in, making Spring laugh and put her arm around Gina, who flinched. Moira had been right: Spring was cold, colder than Wakulla Springs in the middle of January, but, as with a dip in any winter spring, after the initial shock, you could barely feel the chill. Gina savored the coolness against her skin, and the girls sang the rest of their march down the abandoned road of the legendary housing development.

* * *

When the first house appeared, they all stopped and stared.

"So not all the houses got sunk, huh?" Moira looked over Spring's head at Gina. "Told you that story was shit."

Gina should have been relieved to see such irrefutable proof that all the stories about Hawk Point were bullshit, that of course a whole neighborhood didn't fall into the earth. Yet the dilapidated, boarded-up ranch house failed to give any comfort whatsoever, the scaling paint on its face reminding her of a peeling poison-ivy rash. Gaunt cypress saplings poked out of the jungle where its front yard had been, and, as they came abreast with it, they saw a live oak had pitched through the side wall.

"If you knew, why didn't you say?" Gina asked Spring.

She shrugged. "You were half-right, anyway, about them condemning the place. Ground must have been too soft to even bring in machinery to tear these wrecks down."

"We are so going in there," said Moira, already moving up the driveway when Spring grabbed her arm.

"After. First we do the sinks, then you can play house. C'mon," said Spring, hooking Gina with her other cold-ass arm and dragging both girls away from the house.

Moira cackled, then pointed at another house that was coming into sight through the trees. "Dibs on that one. You bring housewarming swag, I *might* let your sorry asses come over for tea and croquet."

"Then I get the next one," said Gina, trying to force herself into the spirit of things. It had worked before—sometimes she just needed to push herself a little to find the fun. Soon enough, though, she regretted claiming an estate sight unseen.

At the end of the third driveway of Hawk Point, all that remained of the house were a few foundations poking up on the rim. They looked like the gravestones Gina had been too chickenshit to spray paint a few weeks ago. Beyond them, beneath them, the sink waited.

Unlike most sinkholes the girls swam in, there was little greenery flanking the sides of the pit, just red clay. It was roughly circular, maybe fifty feet across, and couldn't be more than a ten-foot drop down to the water, but Gina felt dizzy looking over the broken driveway's concrete lip. The water was crystal clear, and, at the right angle, you could see—way, way down—the house's roof, with waterweed columns rising from its moldering shingles. Despite herself, Gina leaned the slightest bit further, looking for the cave that supposedly linked this sink to others in the area, and eventually the river, but the sheer walls of the pit were too dark to tell.

Two hands hit Gina in the small of her back, hard. She stumbled forward but caught herself, and there was a desperate moment where her breath caught and her stomach lurched and her head went light, the toes of her boots rocking on the rough edge of the driveway, and she was going to balance herself, she was...

No. She was too scared to move, and, as if she were a helpless prisoner in her own body, she felt her weight shift, felt the driveway betray her, offering her up as a sacrifice as she toppled—.

Spring grabbed her shirt and jerked her backwards, and Gina collapsed onto the driveway. The sounds of Moira laughing and Spring cursing at Moira were muffled by the sudden ringing that filled Gina's ears. When she caught her breath, she faked a laugh, but even she could tell it sounded off and desperate. Another Doral didn't help, but it did give her something to flick at Moira once she stopped shaking enough to properly aim it.

"Oh dude, what a fuckin' waste!" Moira had side-stepped the missile, and stared forlornly down to where it had sizzled out in the sink. "How many more do we have?"

"Last one," said Gina as Spring helped her up. "I could've cracked my head on the cement, you dumb broad."

"I wasn't really going to let you fall," said Moira. "Probably."

"We've all got to go in on our own," said Spring, by way of arbitration. "But we're all going in."

"Man, even if I wanted to, which I don't, there's no way to get out," said Gina, gesturing at the sink. "Look how steep the sides are. You'd need a rope to climb out, and I don't see any."

"Huh." Moira nodded. "There's probably one tied on a tree or something. Let's look around and see if we can find it."

"We don't need one," said Spring, but accompanied Gina anyway as she took the left side and Moira went right, inspecting the oaks and elms that were near the rim. They reconvened on the far side, where the undergrowth was even thicker.

"No rope means no rope swing," said Moira. "And no rope swing means bullllllshit sink."

"That's probably why they call it Suicide," said Gina. "You'd have to be self-harmy jumping into a sink you couldn't get out of."

"Oh, there's a way out," said Spring slyly. "A bunch of 'em, probably, but we only need one."

"Huh?"

"Get ready, then take a deep breath and follow me," said Spring. When Gina took a step back from the sink, Spring grinned. "Don't worry, I'm not pushing you in. I told you, we all go in on our own. But first, hold your breath on three. One. Two. Three."

As soon as they all took in their lungfuls, Spring began plowing straight through the tangle of thin vines and spiky devil's walking sticks. Moira let Gina push after her, more than happy to let them clear the path a bit, then followed. Her chest had only just begun to hurt when Moira straightened up from her bent walk through the undergrowth and gasped, Spring stepping aside so Gina could join them.

They stood on the bank of a second sink, one entirely enclosed by the nearly impenetrable push of greenery. It was much smaller than the first, with cypress knees jutting out of the gently sloping bank of black mud that angled down to its mirror-still surface. Instead of a nauseating depth, this sink looked to be barely a dozen feet deep and narrow, before it curved into algae-softened rock.

"Oh no," said Gina. "Oh fuck no. Spring, there's no way you can do this. No fucking way."

"You held your breath the whole way," said Spring. "I was listening. And if a smokestack like you can do it, then—"

"Walking a few feet in the woods with my breath held is a lot fucking different than swimming through a cave! It'll be dark down there; you won't see where you're going."

"There's a rope," countered Spring, her bemusement at Gina's reaction fermenting into something nastier. "It goes from one end to the other. You just grab a hold and follow it to the end."

"And if you drop it? Or if it's rotten and falls apart?"

"Then they find you in the river in a few weeks," said Moira quietly. "Dude, I don't think this is such a hot idea."

"The guys I came out here with last night did it. Twice." Spring crossed her arms. "And it was dark as shit, so they didn't even have that going for them. When you get to the end, the cave splits, and you'll be able to see the right way to go from the light. Just drop the rope and kick your way out fast. Besides, there's a spot about halfway through where the roof of the cave opens up and you can surface and breathe, then go the rest of the way."

"Man, what?" For a change, Moira looked to Gina for support. "What if those dudes didn't really swim it, but were pranking you somehow? Seeing if they could trick you into jumping in? You said it was dark, so maybe they tricked you, made it look like—"

"No," said Gina, feeling like a total dumbass for not seeing it sooner. "No, she's right. She knows."

"Huh?" Moira glanced back and forth between her friends. "How can she be sure?"

"She's sure because she already swam it," said Gina, feeling sick to her stomach. She imagined Spring squirming blindly through sunken tunnels, her breath going bad in her chest, her fingers clinging to a slimy rope tethered to the cave walls. Stupid, *stupid* goddamn Spring. "Last night, when you came out here. Those guys swam it, so you swam it after them. That's how you know."

"Half-right, as usual," said Spring smugly. "Those pussies who took me out here were too scared to get in, so I swam it myself."

The woods were loud, and something small splashed back in the first sink. The girls looked at one another. Moira spoke first, her voice heavy with doubt.

"You said you were waiting for us. Why'd you... why didn't you wait? Why'd you bullshit us about it?"

"One look at these sinks, and I knew Gina would have a heart attack if I tried it in front of her bitch ass, and that you'd be too scared to jump in, too. This way I made sure for us, for *all* of us, so we could come back and do it together without worrying."

Moira chewed her lip, and Gina followed suit. Spring had that weird frail look to her that had freaked Gina out so much before, as if maybe she wasn't quite as badass as everybody assumed. Gina felt something rich and thick—an awareness—pushing through her, almost as if her blood was congealing in her veins. All this time Gina had been psyching herself out, letting a bunch of bullshit urban legends and her imagination harsh her calm as she played tough, when all along Spring was the one who was scared. Not just scared, goddamn petrified! And of what? That her closest friends wouldn't think she was a badass unless she did something suicidally stupid?

Awareness turned to awakening, and Gina let it out, then, the wildness that only her friends could unlock in her, and the feeling of unbridled craziness was ecstatic. The undergrowth ripped at her clothes as she dashed back the way they'd come, the heat and humidity almost electric against her skin as she teetered on the edge of the first sink, almost tumbling in when she burst from the ivy and thorns. Her flannel and boots came off in a rush, before she could chicken out, and then the bra she didn't really need yet, but she left her black shirt on. Moira and Spring caught up, howling encouragement, and she stumbled out of her jeans and socks.

With a whoop, Gina launched herself clumsily into the air. She looked up breathless into the sky. The daily thunderstorms were rolling in.

And just like that Gina came back to herself, suspended in the air over the sunken house, and she screamed as the enormity of what she'd committed herself to struck her like a sucker punch. Then she fell, the walls of the sinkhole lunging up to swallow her whole. She hit the clear water and sank halfway down to the house, then kicked up, heart pinballing around her chest. Just before she surfaced she saw the black mouth of the cave set in the wall of the sink, an equally black cable floating in front of its maw like some deep sea creature's lure. Breaking the surface, she was set to beg Moira and Spring to break into a house and find some rope to haul her up when the other two girls hit the water on either side of her.

"Can't do it," Gina chattered, hating how her teeth were rattling despite the water's warmth.

Even treading water was difficult with the sodden shirt pulling her down, but Gina was reluctant to take it off, even when she noticed the other girls were skinny-dipping. Spring usually wore a bikini instead of underwear for just such occasions, but not this time, apparently. Gina's surprise at seeing them naked only distracted her from their predicament for a moment, before the horror of their situation reasserted itself. "Can't do it. Can't."

"Sure you can," said Spring. "You just…"

Then she was gone, flipping around and diving deep. She went into the cave without even bothering to grab the rope, and Gina groaned.

"This was your idea," Moira said fiercely, dog-paddling over to Gina. "I figured you knew some other way out!"

"Noooo," Gina felt herself getting sick, she was going to puke right here, but people couldn't throw up and swim at the same time, could they? She was going to drown mid-puke and—.

"Easy as that!" Spring called from just above them, and Gina looked up to see Spring standing atop the buckled driveway, sleek and shining and outlined by the dirty brown clouds gathering at her back. "Hurry up, everyone out of the pool. Storm's a-comin'!"

Moira laughed and splashed Gina, who could only tread water and gape up at Spring. It had only seemed like a couple of seconds since she dived down into the cave—she must have really lost her shit for a minute there. Gina felt her cheeks flush, and wondered how many people drowned because they wigged themselves out for no reason.

"I'm next!" said Moira, because Moira was always next, and Gina felt her fear return as her friend bobbed over to the edge of the sink above the cave. "I just follow the rope, right?"

"All the way to the end, babe," said Spring. "Halfway through you come up in a cave, so take time to catch your breath there before you go the rest of the way. From there you should be able to see the light from the other cave, so just follow it out. But don't let go of the rope, just in case!"

"Be careful," said Gina, and then Moira was gone.

"I'll wait for her over at the other end, make sure she doesn't stay down too long," said Spring, and before Gina could embarrass herself by asking Spring to stay with her instead, the other girl was gone. Gina began counting, both to take her mind off the fact that she was paddling above a house that was probably full of dead people and also to see how long it took Moira to pass through. Last time Spring had bothered timing them, Gina and Moira could both hold their breath for about a minute, so even if Moira rested for five at the halfway cave she should be out in seven...

At eight minutes, Gina began to freak out.

At nine, she was almost hyperventilating.

At halfway to ten, she started screaming for Spring, Moira, the cops, anyone.

And then Moira poked her head out from behind

an oak at the lip of the sink, her teeth shining even in the half-light of the brewing storm. Spring emerged from the other side of the tree, her jacked-up smile also taunting Gina. At first Gina couldn't say anything, then she didn't want to. Neither Spring nor Moira said anything, just looked down at her as the raindrops began to dimple the water and thunder echoed from back out on the highway.

"Fuck you guys," said Gina, meaning it like she'd never meant it before, and, shimmying out of the cloying shirt, she dived.

The rope was thick and slimy, but there didn't seem to be much give on it. Staring into the darkness of the cave entrance, Gina felt the sudden need to kick back up and get another lungful or a hundred, maybe beg her friends to go for help…but then their condescending smiles flashed through her mind, and, closing her eyes, Gina sunk her fingernails into the rope and pulled herself into the cave.

Every time she pulled herself forward, Gina banged a shoulder or hip on slick stone, but the walls of the cave were never there for purchase when she tried to kick herself faster along. The air in her lungs turned bad and she pushed it out, trying not to let the reality of where she was and what she was doing take hold. Her chest went from tingling to hot to a furnace, and then she felt light-headed, her limbs itching. She was going to black out.

She swam faster, letting go of the rope and opening her eyes in the hope that she could catch some glint of daylight to make for. Instead, she saw a soft glow emanating from…a TV? She had drifted into a retro living room occupied by lounging skeletons in fish-eaten board shorts and bikinis watching a busted, waterlogged television. In the middle of this family, Spring and Moira sat on the couch, their hair floating above their faces like halos. Gina gasped and swallowed water, making her body convulse against this inevitable drowning. She jetted mute screams. She didn't want to drown. She didn't even want to dive in the first place. She—

Surfaced with a gasp. Gina coughed up water and gulped the stale, moist oxygen, reveling in the way it burned her lungs. She had made it. The halfway cave.

"Gina? Is that you?"

Gina's legs and arms cramped at the sound of Moira's voice. What the fuck was she doing here? Why would she swim back in—they could have collided in the dark, or become stuck, or—.

A faint light poured down with the rain pelting Gina's face, and, with its illumination, she saw Moira treading water with a load. She was clinging to a vague lump of driftwood. Other than Moira and the undulating surface of the underground lake, Gina couldn't see shit.

"Ginaaaaa!" Moira shrieked, her voice echoing in the shadows.

"It's me," Gina panted, paddling closer to Moira, and, it seemed, the light. "Why'd you swim back down?"

"What? Oh, God! What's fucking happening?" Moira splashed around, struggling with her make-shift buoy. She thrust it from her body, sobbing as it bobbed further into the light. Gina saw Spring's hay-colored hair completely cleansed of its cherry-flavored dye, and then her friend's face came into sight as the body slowly rotated in the water, re-vealing a bluish, bloated face.

"I found her as soon as I came up here, but what the fuck—she's supposed to be up top! I saw her, she made it!" Moira's voice broke, and Gina felt the panic in her friend's voice infect her even as she looked away from the corpse, telling herself it wasn't really there. They had both just seen Spring, and she was fine. Before Gina could reflexively tell Moira it was okay, even though it definitely wasn't, something fell, splashing her in the face. Gina looked up and saw where the light was coming from: a small circle of pale light was above them, with two smaller circles of darkness limned against its border. Faces, peering down, the rain drizzling around them. Gina's eyes burned, and, rubbing them with her knuckles, she squinted up. Spring looked down at her. Next to her was Moira, poised to throw another rock down.

"Spring? Moira?" Gina looked back to her friends and saw they were still in the water beside her, one treading water, the other...

Gina turned her eyes back to the hole above them. She was in shock, that was what was up, somebody was fucking with them, and she was in shock, but that was no excuse to act stupid. She had to be practical.

"Look," Gina called. "I don't know who you fuckers are, but we've had enough of your bullshit. Throw us some rope! Call the cops! This isn't funny anymore." Gina paddled around, stretching her toes to find something solid to rest on. Nothing but warm water. She cocked her head up to petition their tormentors anew but choked when she saw another girl peek down the tunnel. It was herself; Gina waved down at Gina.

"Gina?" Moira whimpered.

"What?" Gina's sudden dizziness caused her to sink completely under, and she surfaced clumsily, trying not to throw up. "*What?!*"

"I think I know why Spring was so cold earlier."

"Oh the fuck you do. You better keep swimming,

Moira! You hear me? Swim until help comes." Gina angrily splashed water onto Moira's face, but the other girl didn't even flinch, her eyes wide. She was clinging to Spring again, the drowned one, and her fingers were digging so deep into their friend's pale shoulder that black ooze was leeching out.

"You bitches!" Gina yelled up the cave. "Who the fuck are you?!"

Spring, the Spring in the world above, where the rain fell but would stop in an hour, leaving everything steaming in the summer sunshine, laughed, and her laughter echoed and bounced off the water, rattling through Gina's ears. The three girls disappeared, but Gina heard them singing Moira's version of "Dive." Gina, *the real Gina*, she told herself, joined in, trying to keep her shit together, but pretty soon she grew tired and just listened. The light was fading, or maybe the hole above them was receding, and Gina's weary limbs barely carried her over to where Moira clung to Spring's heavy, bobbing body.

"Dive! Dive! Dive! Dive with me!"

The singers grew distant, their song trailing away in the deepening dark, and then the cave went silent, save for the occasional splash and thrash from whatever was still alive within it. Up above, on the empty, desolate rim of the sink, the only sound was the pattering of rain on the surface of the water.

Collaborative Disambiguation

with Virginia M. Mohlere

I.

Quixote: El Dorado Hampered by Evil Magicians

LA MANCHA: In a news conference today, a spokesman for Don Quixote announced that the Don has received intelligence that evil magicians are hampering the spread of Lady Dulcinia of El Dorado's treasures among the people. "They work in secret, all over," the spokesman said. "These magicians could be your neighbors. The war against them is a war we all need to fight. Keep your eyes open and your pike ready." Don Quixote was unavailable for comment.

On the stock market, drubbings are up 1¾, hot meals are holding steady, and soft beds are down 4.7%.

* * *

Virginia and I both liked crusades, and the idea of Don Quixote, and did not like the war or current politics. We realized our dislikes and likes shared a common bond worthy of an epic poem.

Giddy, we agreed to concoct a work of collaboration. I was pursuing a dream in a very real, and crappy, journalist job, meanwhile trying to come to terms with a new city that was probably the most uninspiring place on earth. I don't dare call it hell, because as we all know, hell has many muses. In the back of my mind was always our project—a new Don Quixote that would ridicule the GOP.

II.

I had my own upheavals: my sweet telecommuting gig ended, and I was faced with the choice of (1) losing all my benefits or (2) heading from Texas to Chicago to live in a series of guest rooms, 1000 miles away from my husband. At the beginning of that adventure, I imagined that I'd spend my commuting hours writing on the train. Selena and I would have a ball: I imagined a work that would be funny and a little romantic. I was going to take the Sancho voice, and I was eager to get on it.

Then it occurred to me that perhaps a love of *The Man of La Mancha* would not quite be an adequate foundation for our project. I borrowed a copy of *Don Quixote* and got reading. If you haven't read it, do. But round about Book 2, when it starts to go meta on itself, the enormity of my rootlessness hit me, and all the creativity fell out of my head. It made a wet sort of sound when it hit the pavement. Writing on the train: ha! Apparently I need two things to write: adequate sleep and a sense of safety. I kept trying to write, and it was like picking a scab. It really sucks to have a great idea and no wherewithal to work on it.

* * *

Cervantes could understand that. Traveling from one town to the other in the pursuit of financial success, for twenty years he only produced a handful of titles. It was not until he was jailed for tax evasion that the man had a moment to comfortably roost in his brain. Thus, Don Quixote was born. I would not say jail provided him with a sense of safety, but it gave him enough solitude and boredom to listen to his thoughts, enough withdrawal from the world that only saw windmills for Cervantes to show Quixote they were giants.

We were having the problem of seeing the wind-mills for what they were.

III.

Boredom! It sounds positively blissful. The soli-tude to roost in my own mind, head tucked down into my neck feathers, cooing to myself in the dark. In Texas, I grumbled about the lack of adventures and longed for the smell of concrete and exhaust. I got my adventure, boy howdy.

How do you tell when the windmill is your own manufacture? Does that even matter?

The Chivalrous War

Thousands of miles from La Mancha,
Myriad Sanchos survey the desert,
Belligerently bedighted to defend their Lady
Upon Sir Quixote's command...

It is said Dulcinia's blood percolates from the soil
And can fuel even the wildest dreams,
But for the Sanchos their only wish
Is for her powers to transport them back home.

But first they must find the road she now roams,
Lady Dulcinia, of El Dorado,
And when they find her, they can only admire her,
And cannot touch an ounce of her City of Gold.

They must take pleasure in the fortune she has given
To Quixote, and hope, that one day, it will trickle down
Into a small fortune of their own.

* * *

My windmills are not giants but palm-trees, blowing purposefully in the wind.

Boredom. How dreadful. Locked away in a house with white walls and linoleum floors, where I can't communicate with the fence-pissing neighbors next door...breaking news is an added wing of the hospital.... The only existential retreat is the beach, and having lived ten miles from the beach, let me tell you, you don't go as much as you would think. There is work, there is home, there is food and sleep. Boredom is supposed to be the gales that set into motion electricity...yet, boredom has become my downfall, my routine, my coveted downtime of being.

What was supposed to be adventurous was as glum and lame as the old Don's dusty library.

The collaboration with Virginia was a salve. Not having one relatable person to speak with in my new surroundings, our correspondence was chemical, encouraging, and therapeutic. We were two minds, linked together with a vision that sometimes wrote itself without our having muttered one word to the other...*Dulcinia, Dulcinia, Dul-ci-nia.*

But without the conversation, our vision wilted

in the real world, and merely wandered before us as Aldonza.

IV.

Isn't that the story of so many artistic endeavors? In your mind it's Dulcinia: it's poignant and resonant. But the work, when it's done, is a mere Aldonza. I've dreamed whole novels before, and although I might remember the entire story arc when I wake, I have never been satisfied with the writing. It's never as *enough* as it is in my sleep. As I dream. (Of course the artist's dream is the perfect story/painting/dance/etc.)

Sometimes I think: is it better to embrace the Aldonzas? Is it better to embrace the blowsy, flawed things that come out of the pen? But let's face it: I just can't let my whole writing life be silly poems about history set to the meter of TV themes.

God, I hope not, anyway.

I spent months ragging on myself for not collaborating with Selena, and it turns out that we were collaborating all along: we were moving along the same path, separated by who knows how many miles, both of us following the glint of gold in the distance but too often distracted by the gravel underfoot.

What I hope for my collaborator is for her El Dorado to find her—or at least, for her to never stop looking for it. Maybe that gravel has some gold in it. I guess I won't find out unless I keep digging. May it ever be so.

The United States of Kubla Khan

I was walking in downtown Tallahassee this evening, and found an extension cord laying on the sidewalk. Curious, I followed the neon orange snake several blocks into what seemed an abandoned basement. Upon entering, I found in the darkness a young brunette, curled up in a ball on a black futon, bug-eyes glued to CNN. Her pallor was deathly from flashing Ben Day, but her contracting irises acknowledged she was alive. I knelt down beside her, turning on my most southern of charms.

"Good evening, Miss. I didn't mean to intrude but I was curious about this extension cord." She said nothing. "Uh, I'm M.T. Gonzaga, perhaps you've read my columns?" I flashed my press badge, holding it up in her face. Without averting her gaze from the TV, she monophonically muttered, "I am the Last American Dreamer."

Ha, aren't we all? I thought. But my skepticism yielded to my journalistic sixth sense; there might be a story here, or at least a bit of fun. I got out my tape-recorder.

"American Dreamer," I said, trying to sound professional and not titter. "Do you envision this new America as being stronger, more progressive in its attempts at Democracy?" With a terse grunt, her arms and legs shot out and began to writhe as her entire body convulsed. Her eyes, jiggling in their sockets, tried to focus on the ceiling. I could have called 9-1-1, but there was no phone in the place, and my cell laid on a Holiday Inn nightstand. So I braced her arms and applied pressure to her body, trying to calm her down.

When she stopped shaking, I knelt down by her face, and decided to pour four words, like poison, down her ears: "What do you dream?"

Her torso shot straight-up, her hair whipping me in the face. I could hear sound bubbling in her throat.

"I dream?" she finally muttered. "No, no, I *dreamt!*" There was silence as her head seemed to traverse the moldings of the room. She paused upon a teddy bear wearing an American Flag sweater, and she gasped, speaking the rest of the monologue in an air-sucking manner.

"I dreamt people would forgo the Prodigal Son for minds capable of speaking outside of Comic Book cant and would consider the lives of his citizens and the weight of Truth over his tarnished Gold." She raised her hand, curled it around an imaginary re-mote-control, and began channeling her thoughts with her thumb.

"People would think for themselves and not solely within the context of religion or fear of mythology. While Jihads are threats to our national security, Crusades are threats to our National identity." *Click.*

"Of an enlightened Superpower that would rec-ognize and apologize for its mistakes and truly learn from those same errors. Not a President who jigs and winks at the hysterically applauding few." *Click.*

"Of evolving, open dialogue. Before, Americans refused to listen, and now they are deaf, dismissing questions or doubts as terrorist sympathies. Now, being American means washing your mouth out with the Constitution, not reading it." She shook her head and made spitting noises, her hands clambered at her tongue, and once the imaginary thing was taken out she: *Click.*

"Of never having to be Political, of trusting the

words of the Elected, reading the Founding Fathers for inspiration, rather than primary sources for street-side debate." She paused, a look of ecstasy melted onto her face.

"Of an economy that would accept me with open arms." She put the "remote" down to wrap her arms around her tiny shoulders and her face became quite irate. Her whispers crescendoed in anger.

"That Legislators would acknowledge that socializing Healthcare won't make them, or the nation, Red-Pinko-Commie-Fascists; that everyone wants the right to life, liberty, and happiness, not sickness, confinement, and wretchedness.

"Of unquestioned equality and unconditional understanding of people by the People. Yet 'Muslim' is the new derogative as 'Negro' was in the 60s, 'Feminist' was in the 70s, and 'Gay' was in the 90s. I dreamt that there would be an end to new derogatives and that freedom's domestic enemy wasn't pursuance of happiness. That from this Huxley-knockoff nation I could go into the world—vivid, alive, awake, and vital—proud of the populace that I, by chance alone, was born into." She stopped and fell backwards into the hard futon, eyes rolling back into her head.

Bewildered by this automatic manifesto, I stared at this inanimate creature, the zombie on the futon writhing to the words of Wolf Blitzer on the screen.

I stopped my tape-recorder, and wondered whether I should call the Smithsonian? No, D.C. would kill her, then it would all be gone, this last grain of sand from the shore of endless tides. Everything has been washed away, except this delirious vegetable in a dark basement watching stolen cable.

And right she is—what role is left for a dreamer? Poet? Activist? Diplomat? Economist? Who listens to these people anymore? Everyone has become deaf, afraid of the *quid pro status quo*.

Dreamers are talkers, and talk is cheap; a *de trop* commodity in an economy based on debt. If the American people can afford it, they don't want it. There is no climb in status if one lives within their means, and in our land of equality that's what we're concerned with: being better than everyone else. So, even in the cosmopolitan (more juice than vodka) of Tallahassee, no one will bother to preserve the Last American Hope—comatose on a futon, fetalized by the media, speechless in the face of fear and nationalistic fervor—because her words are not ticker symbols, her dreams are not timeshares, but visions of a democracy, unwrapped in greed and image, and adorned in love and ingenuity.

Her attention had focused upon me during my reveries. She almost looked normal, or serene at least, when my eyes met hers. She smiled sadly.

"The wind cannot carry words," and her eyes grew heavy and shut.

What would happen to her? Would a realtor, ten years from now, salivating from another boom, stumble upon her skeleton, her shallow bug-eyes vacantly staring at Soledad O'Brien desperately trying to fathom the occurrence of Revelations on our soil?

I grew angry. I felt responsible. I was a journalist, like these clowns, and the integrity of my field morphed and lessened with the copulation of their brand of reporting: contriving every serious occurrence into sequestered drama, so that no one will look too close, no one will fear to stay tuned for the next national disaster. So common has this "Crying Wolf" hysteria become, that no one will read objective facts, every story must have a hero and a villain, and always a Christian moral spin. But somehow, this girl could read between every word—and the loneliness of that fact was making her insane.

But what could I do? I couldn't force her to go out into this world she fears, nor could I tell her it was getting any better, that her dreams would materialize.

Watching her sleep, I tiptoed to the television and found where it connected to the extension cord. I gently unplugged it, and wrapped the extension cord around my elbow—following it out the door, just as

I had followed it in. I took one last look at the Last American Dreamer, but the basement, robbed of its only light source, was as dark as a catacomb. It enshrouded her in shadow, and only an impression of her umbrous silhouette, and her slumbering breath remained.

Vintage Scenes #2:

2010 Bernkasteler Lay Riesling Spätlese

1.

If there is anything wine teaches us, it is that you are never satisfied with where you are while you are there, nor with what you have. Pleasures are always trapped within the past—the present is for forgetting and Spring is ephemeral, despite what they say.

Blame the senses. Long after the brain has reset and erased itself of daily minutiae, including details once thought sublime, the senses recover the data and through smell and taste reboot the soul into yearning for this place that has developed behind dark room retinas from buried negatives.

Even when you are sunbathing in 95 degree weather on some panhandle shore with periwinkle skies and plump sfumato clouds drifting over the oscillating teal Gulf, the uncorking of the Spätlese releases a chill only felt at the turn of the vernal equinox, and the crisp, floral palette transports you across the sea and into the fairy tale valley of Bavaria where mad kings built fantasies in the mountains for the imagined fey.

Even the jade bottle connotes season. Goethe thought green, and its hues and tints, the most relaxing and comforting color in the spectrum, and perhaps that is because all of Bavaria seems cloaked in a verdant palette. Spring's vessel reminds you of this; the bottle has the muted blue shade akin to the distant alps reflected in the lakes along the Romantic Road.

You miss that scenery, even though while you witnessed it you craved vignettes of home.

2.

And who do you have to thank for this? Baudelaire? Rimbaud? Poe? No, a miscommunication at the Alpenrose Am Se in Hohenschwangau.

You were killing time until the Schloss Neuschwanstein tour, nursing a weak and cold espresso, when the waiter asked you if you wanted anything else. Your mouth chiseled Deutsch pebbles that were suppose to say: "I don't know. The tour is soon, won't I be late?" The waiter nodded and dashed off and returned with a glass of chamomile colored wine instead of a check. "Spätlese," is all he said before dashing off to another table. Completely flummoxed by the obvious miscommunication, you slouched in your chair and considered the glass.

The wine was the golden blanch of a dried dandelion bud and smelled of displeasing acetone and fetid fruit. Even so, you tasted it. Apples, white grapes, pears, and honeysuckle swirled on your tongue; the acetone stink faded into an alpine note.

You felt cold and clean like the air in the valley, but when you closed your eyes you longed for the blinding and blistering sun and imagined dead leaves mixed with azalea, dogwood, magnolia, pear, and trumpet honeysuckle petals blowing in a silent whirlwind down oak-lined streets. You knew you were missing the best parts of home in bloom and grew melancholy that you'd have to wait another year to enjoy it.

Lost in rumination, you realized you were late to the tour, and throwing money over your shoulder you jogged a mile up a ninety-degree trail only to arrive at the Neuschwanstein gates asphyxiated and access denied. It should not have been such an arduous trek, but your lungs somehow were made heavy by the Riesling and the elevation and the view. It was the first time you were aware of your own breathing.

3.

Back home on the shore, you gasp the humid air after each sip of the Spätlese trying to reclaim that same breathlessness not even found when emerging from a long dive.

But it is pointless. No matter where you are, you always want your breath taken away without appreciating the fact that you are still breathing at all.

The Last Session

"Mom. Mom! Look at me, okay. I think I can do what Dr. Gonzaga does. Just...watch it twirl, okay?... Alright, Mom, ready? Then let us begin.

"Behold my pendulum, watch it spin as it calibrates the rhythms of our world. Right now, you are without by being within—you, too, must be calibrated. From the beginning or the end, follow your gravitation.

"Now, Mom, I want you to breathe deeply. Slowly. When you exhale, imagine you are blowing the pain out of your body. Now look within, and without losing focus on the breath, tell me about the pain."

"My back...my spine. When I breathe, shards of glass stick—."

"It's okay, Mom. It's okay. Just relax—come back to the breath. You have been in a lot of pain. I want you to visualize your pain. Can you see it?...Mom? Mom, can you see it? The pain?"

"Yes."

"Hold that image in your mind as we breathe the trinity. Inhale through your nose until you feel it in your stomach and hold.

"Inhale now up to the ribs and hold.

"And inhale up to the collar bone and hold.

"Now release the breath through your mouth. And in that exhale, expel the pain from your body and from your mind."

"*Ehhhhheaaaah.*"

"Good, Mom, that's awesome. You are doing awesome. Now repeat three times."

"—.—. —. *Ehhhhheaaaah.* —. —. —. *Ehhhh-heaaaah.* —. —. —.*"

"Exhale one more time. You gotta do it three times, you only did it twice. Breathe it all out. Come on, Mom, breathe it all out!"

"...don't want...leave you...clahreezzah."

"You're not, Mom. It's just the pain. Pain is only

within the body."

"lahreezzah."

"It distracts the mind and burdens the soul, sending the body into internal war. When you can master the body with the mind, the soul becomes strong and—*Shit, what was that word Dr. Gonzaga used? supernal? supernatural?*—sempiternal.

"You have mastered the body with your mind today, and unburdened by earthly pain, your soul will again reign. I am about to awake your soul with the sphere, and when you feel it pierced and pinched into dominance, I want you to awake.

"Mom. Listen. When I snap, you will awake. The pain will still be gone but you gotta wake up."

Snap—

"Leeeeeeeeave..."

Snap—

"Leeeeeeeeave...."

Snap.

"lahreezzah."

"Mom? You awake? Mom, I snapped! Wake up!"

PART ONE

The bathroom, again. I lay splayed on the broken and mildewed tile. You dangled an O.B. tampon over my face. It was the only object on a string you could find, and the doctor said anything would do. I remember she told you that. An innocent response to an innocent question now made retroactively ominous.

My robe was open, breasts exposed, shriveled and dimpled like rotted orange peels. I never wanted you to see me like this, but this was the scene you'd been witnessing for months, ever since the first time you discovered me in the bathroom, in this exact same manner. Confronted with my fragility, you had never seen me so vulnerable. You wanted to call 911, but I'd come to in time to prevent it and all the bills that would have come after.

We couldn't afford this. While I made enough to keep our household afloat, there wasn't enough money for luxuries like medical emergencies or precautions against them. Plus, I didn't really want to know what was wrong with me. I didn't want you to know. I was afraid it would change things—make them too hard— but it was too late. I was no longer secure.

It was inevitable, I realized, and the only way to maintain control was to become cruel. I began to lie to you, and with each deceit, I made you watch me die.

I told you, and everyone else, that I was a Christian Scientist. It seemed to cover all the bases and saved you from other's pity and half-hearted charity. And, for a while, I believed God would heal me. I know you were skeptical, but it explained away the fear by explaining why I was growing thinner and exhausted and not going to the doctor. It explained everything but that we were poor.

Then came the pain, and I dropped the religion schtick for Dr. Gonzaga. No insurance required, I only paid what I could, and she'd let you sit in, too. I thought it'd be educational for you. An opportunity to allow your horizons to broaden while you stayed near.

It helped.

I could see it—the black tumor that stained my blood and threatened to carry me away from you. I watched it spread from my mammary glands into my veins—for months I've watched it—a tentacular mass grasping at my white blood cells. At the end of every session, I'd imagine the cells slipping from its grip, becoming impenetrable, eventually unionizing and devouring the threat until the pain faded away.

This time, though, I watched as the dark malignancy penetrated and passed through them, and the cells collapsed and floated through my bloodstream like dust caught in sunbeams.

Then I felt deflated. I was all breathed out. I floated

through myself, but could not get to the beckoning beyond.

I don't want to leave you, Clarissa. You are still just a child.

Chapter One

"What? Gross."

"No, dude, it was hot. Betcha won't find that in Brontë. Plus, when he eats me out, he spells the alphabet."

"What do you mean?"

"On the clit," Laney looked at Clarissa's furrowed brow.

"Christ, Clarissa, when are you going to stop being such a blushing virgin and get fucked!" Out the window, Clarissa watched the trees blur with the telephone lines and poles.

"So...like...morse code with his tongue or something?"

"No, like licking *around* it."

"Oh."

"But morse code would be good, too. You aren't as hopeless as you seem, you know. You could probably get Jack Calvino to send you a S.O.S with some initiative."

"Yeah, right."

Jack Calvino was Murat High's residential beatnik. With *Dharma Bums* rolled into his thread worn jeans, he wandered the halls jingling the loose change in his pockets, quoting "America."

"Why not? He has a car, right? Get him to skip fifth, take you to Mossy Pond and start tapping on his knee." Laney reached over to demonstrate and Clarissa slapped her hand away.

"Is that where your daddy bad touched?"

"Naw, ain't got one. Must have been yours."

Laney slammed on the breaks to avoid rear-ending a sudden-breaker.

"Fucking dipshit!" She looked over her shoulder and swerved around the slow-crawling Buick, rolling down her window to shoot the driver a bird. Clarissa looked through the back window.

"Laney, that was someone's grandma!"

"It could be my grandma for all I care. Get the fuck out of the way!"

"She can't hear you. The window's back up."

"Take the wheel."

"What?" The car began to swerve into the next lane as Laney hiked her skirt to take off her tights.

"Take the wheel! These things itch like crazy." Clarissa grabbed it and steadied the car. "Jesus, Laney."

"What? Nothing happened." She threw the tights over her shoulder into the backseat. She relieved Clarissa of the wheel and grabbed a cigarette from out of the arm rest.

"You still not smoking?" Clarissa shook her head. Laney shrugged and lit the cigarette. "Listen, Miss-Chri-Sci-Monitor, we're all gonna die from something."

Clarissa winced and returned to window-gazing, while Laney kept on: "Shit, you could do it tonight if you could get out from under your mom. Just find him after his set and go straight for ego, total groupie style."

"Yeah...I'm not doing that."

"Come on. What are you afraid of? Besides everything."

"I'm not a fucking groupie."

"Ah, I get it. You forgot to shave." Laney began cackling at the shocked look on Clarissa's face. "Jeezus, get your head out of the Brontë, girl. You know the story about Ruskin's honeymoon night, right? Dudes have no idea what really goes on down there. Read some Sade or something, hell, Nin or Colette. Acker? Something! How can you be into punk rock and read nothing but that proper shit all day?"

"If you ever actually read a book and didn't Cliff Note it like I know you do, you'd realize that the whole point of the Ruskin story isn't that we should shave, it's that the idea of beauty is completely subjective upon the male's gaze. He saw paintings with no pubes all the time, and so thought all women had bald pussy. But, the men had bald balls in the paintings and sculptures too, and don't you bet Ruskin didn't shave his hairy balls or think twice about them when he jacked it looking at Venus—." Clarissa sucked the rest of her thesis back into her lungs. "Besides, what more do I need to learn with a nympho friend like you?"

"Nice." Laney finally kept her eyes on the road.

Satisfied, Clarissa turned up the radio and The Dismemberment Plan's "Girl O'Clock" filled up the silence Clarissa's burn left. She started hitting the top of the car in beat to the song until Laney joined in and they sang along until they pulled up to Clarissa's apartment complex and parked the car.

"Seriously though, it's too bad your mom won't let you go to the show."

"Yeah, I know. I'd really like to go and see the bands."

"Well, why don't you?"

"What do you mean?"

"Clarissa, you are sixteen years old. How long are you going to let your mommy tell you what to do? It's about time wittle Clawissa starts making decisions for herself. Sneak out. What's the worst that could happen?"

"Fuck you, Laney." She pushed the image of her mother splayed out on the tile from her mind. "You know it's different than with your folks. Besides, how would I get there?"

"Hello! Are you not being transported by Laney Cabs as we speak?"

"The show will be over by the time—."

"Not tonight. I've been saving the best intel for last, my virgin queen. There's going to be a house show after the hootenanny...and do you want to know whose house?" Laney tapped Clarissa's knee a few times exhaling smoke out of a salacious smirk.

"I just don't really see how—."

"Just think about it. I'll be home getting ready until 6:30. Call me before then, and let me know if you want me to come get you." Laney dragged on her cigarette and looped her arm on the wheel as Clarissa dragged all her shit out of the car. When Clarissa stuck her head back in to give Laney a hug, Laney shrinked back.

"I don't get it, Clarissa. Why doesn't she just go to a doctor and do chemo or whatever like everyone else?"

Clarissa shrugged. "She just doesn't."

"But like...she has to...at some point...doesn't she? It's not really fair to you."

"Just...call me later and tell me about the show, okay?"

Clarissa shut the door and walked towards the apartment complex. She looked back to watch Laney drive off into another night of possibilities.

She ascended the stairs, and saw Mr. Argenziano on the stoop, smoking his fiftieth cigar of the day while watching the comings and goings of the entire complex and creeping it up.

"Sexy weekend with your girlfriend planned?" Clarissa threw her hand up in an idle wave.

"Howse Sarah doin'? I ain't seen her in days. She's sick, right?"

"Yup."

"What's wrong with her?"

"Working on finding that out, Mr. A." Clarissa lied and fumbled for her keys.

"Can't fuck around with stuff like that."

"Sure can't. Thanks for asking. Bye!" Clarissa rushed through the door and tried not to slam it.

"Ugh, why does he have to do that?" Clarissa expected to hear the familiar soft clicks of her mother at the computer in response, but found no one at the desk and the computer off. She threw her keys and bag onto the breakfast nook and beelined it to her mother's room and found her still in bed.

"Hey Mom! You up?" Her mother laid in the same position Clarissa had left her in. Clarissa shook her shoulders and recoiled at how stiff she felt. "Mom?" She held her fingers under the nose, and felt a slight draft passing through the nostrils.

"Hey, Mom, wake up." Her mom's eyes flew open and stared at the ceiling. "Oh, thank God." Clarissa stood up. "How are you doing? Did you get your nap out? Any pain today?" Clarissa's mother continued to stare at the ceiling. "Okay, well, you keep resting and I'll check back in. Do you need anything?" Her mother closed her eyes.

Clarissa headed to her room. To avoid dwelling over the weirdness of that interaction, she wondered about the show. She ruminated over Laney's speculation that she could hook-up with Jack "groupie-style."

A brief fantasy of Jack Calvino dragging her on stage for a Thelma and Louise stage dive flittered through her cranium. She jumped towards the eager beckoning hands and bounced and rolled off of her bed, her ass cracking against the concrete carpeted floor. She laughed at herself and grabbed her guitar, plugged it in, and listened to the feedback before tuning.

She didn't want to just hook up with Jack, she

wanted his attention. She began picking arpeggios then slid into the riff she'd been working on all week. It cleared her brain and made her forget things for the next few hours.

When it was 6 o'clock, Clarissa turned her amp down to listen for her mother's customary knock about dinner, but heard nothing. The house was quiet but for the Palmer's feedback. Clarissa turned it off and threw it on the bed. She went back to see her mother, who was still on her back, unmoved.

"Mom? You up for cooking dinner? Or want me to call take-out or something?" Clarissa's mother's eyes opened to the ceiling again.

"Or I could try and do it...just gotta tell me what to do."

Silence.

"Hey, Mom! Cook dinner?" Her mother threw off the sheets, stood up and walked to the kitchen. Clarissa followed suit and settled into the usual stool at the breakfast bar. She waited for the customary inquiry into her day, but her mother was silent as she gathered frozen bricks of peas and carrots from the freezer.

"So, school was okay today. We talked about Robert Browning, and I think I embarrassed the teacher when I asked why he wasn't mentioning

Elizabeth at all. Can you believe that?" Her mother moved down to the cupboard and searched the canisters for rice.

"Other than that, same ole, same ole. Laney gave me a ride home. She's going to the Thunderdome Hootenanny tonight. Asked me if I could go."

Her mother remained silent and didn't even look up out of her usual agitation when Clarissa asked to go out. She looked normal, or what had become normal over the past few months. Her shirt hung off of her shoulders and Clarissa resisted counting the number of ribs and vertebrae she could see while waiting for her mom to respond.

She wondered whether she should push it after last night.

"Just you know, if I am ever going to be in a band or whatever, it'd be nice to see what the other kids are doing."

Her mother turned her back on Clarissa to stand over the defrosting microwave.

Clarissa sighed and set the table. When her mother finished bringing out the meager dishes, she hovered over the spread and stared at the wall.

"Mom, aren't you going to sit down and eat?" Clarissa's mom sat in her chair, and made her plate; however, she did not eat what was on it, merely stared at it.

"Look, mom, I know I shouldn't have asked, but come on, I can ask. It shouldn't make you so upset with me you won't eat. You need to eat, Mom." Her mother blinked a few times and her eyes focused on the plate. She grabbed her fork and began eating.

Dinner was usually the zenith of her mother's day, so Clarissa was surprised to see her mother have no sensorial reaction to her food. Instead, she went through the motions like an automaton. What was going on with her? At least she wasn't writhing in pain, a small win, but Clarissa wondered how long it would last, and wondered how much worse it would continue to be.

"Mom, you licked the plate clean. Why...uh...why are you still eating?" Her mother was now fishing for unseen fair with her fork. Clarissa watched her lick the bare utensil and repeat the motions several times until she realized her mom must be joking with her.

"Stop it, mom." Clarissa laughed. Her mother dropped the fork in the plate and went back into stare mode.

Clarissa slid out of her chair and walked over to her mom. She waved her hand in front of her mom's face and saw her eyes did not waver.

"Mom. Follow my hand." Her mother shifted and

her eyes began to follow her daughter's hand.

A pattern was beginning to present itself to Clarissa, but she fought against recognizing it in her mind, not understanding what had enacted the patterns to be put in place. Instead, she cleared the table and noticed her mother's eyes continued following her hands as they stacked plates, gathered napkins, and wiped the table down.

"Stop following my hand?" Her mother did as she was commanded. "Go start the dishes?" Her mother rose from her chair and went to the kitchen and began running water into the sink.

Holy shit, Clarissa thought, *is she still hypnotized?*

Clarissa looked at the clock and saw it was 6:20. She grabbed the portable and went into her room to call Laney.

"Hey, good timing, I am just out the door."

"Will you come get me?"

"Seriously?"

"Yeah...seriously."

"Hell yeah, I'll come get you. Just, like, put pillows under the covers and stuff, and maybe she won't notice you are gone." The pang of guilt only lasted for a nanosecond.

"I have something figured out. See you in the

parking lot. Be quiet! No horns."

Clarissa returned to the kitchen just in time to turn the faucet off before the sink overflowed. Just as her mother couldn't stop eating until commanded too, she was washing and rinsing phantom dishes in the flooding basin.

"Stop, stop, stop! Phew, that was close. Now, listen." Clarissa's mother faced her and cocked her head. "I am going to go out with Laney, tonight. You have to let me go. You are going to let me go?" Clarissa wasn't sure how to phrase this as a command. "Give me permission to go." Clarissa watched her mother's distant gaze, waiting for her to snap out of it and possibly slap Clarissa for her insolence. Instead, a bronchial rattle vibrated from her mother's throat and seeped through her lips: "Leeeeeeeeeave."

* * *

When severed from the coil, you learn harsh truths about the lives you leave behind. It's like getting to look up the correct answers after taking a pop-quiz, feeling confident you aced it, only to see in red ink that each and every solution was incorrect.

It had been a mistake. All of it. Not only the dying, but the living. I'd done it all wrong.

My biggest error was to raise you in fear. Your first memories were composed of it, thanks to your father.

And for some reason, at the time you were born, the world had seemed to surrender to evil, even in our own little Mayberry town. As long as I could help it, no daughter of mine would be struck by all of the world's evil. It was best you stayed home where I could keep an eye on you.

It wasn't difficult when you were small. You loved me, and you loved being around me. But, by the sixth grade, when I enrolled you in school, you started making friends and started wanting to "go hang out" with them. I remember the first time you asked if you could go to the mall with Laney, and I responded with: "And get your head cut off and be buried in the woods like Loreli Brand? Out of the question."

"Mom, that was over ten years ago."

"Doesn't matter. It happens every day. Just last week, a woman from Madison was abducted when trying to change a blown tire. People aren't nice like they used to be, Clarissa. You've got to be careful."

Then you began to rebuke me with how other parents acted. That none of them were worried about such things. That your friends got to participate in rites-of-passages every weekend, while you stayed home and read books in your room. I'd tell you I wasn't like those parents, that maybe they didn't love their kids as much as I loved mine, that perhaps they didn't have to fight and work as hard as I did to have you, that with all the books and music I bought you when we could barely afford it, you shouldn't want for stimulation. You should be grateful.

And for the most part, I think you were. Aside from these arguments, you were a good girl—you rarely disobeyed or got in trouble at school and were so damn smart—but now I know this wasn't solely out of gratitude, but out of fear. The fear of repercussions. The fear I raised you within.

In the back of the parenting quiz, it tells me that I overreacted, and rather than make you careful, it made you cruel. A side of you I've never seen before has been revealed. Despite how hard I've tried, you still grow up with or without me.

I feel betrayed—by this world, by this body, by everyone I've ever known. You were all I ever had. I do not want to let you go. I refuse. As long as you still need me, I remain. Even when you ask me to let you go, I remain.

Chapter Two

Clarissa was surprised to find that Jack Calvino lived in a McMansion way out in Killeen, an ex-suburb reserved for the town's middling nouveau riche. Secondhand Volvos, Mercedes, and other import cars parked up and down the cul-de-sac alongside sparkling Jags and BMWs. In the backyard, naked boys wrestled in the darkness or trampolined next to the pool. The girls stood in the corner affecting boredom at the prospect of getting splashed.

"Laney! We thought you'd never come!" one of the girls exclaimed, then the whole gaggle hugged Laney as one, and as one, they stared at Clarissa without offering a hand or any general acknowledgment. Clarissa waited for Laney to make the introductions, but she didn't bother.

"Cobb is inside listening to the show."

"Oh yeah, whose playing right now?"

"A Poison on Her Lips, obviously."

Laney grabbed Clarissa's hand and dragged her towards the house. "We're just in time."

The door opened into a living room—all occupied by standing dudes in black t-shirts and bangs that flopped in measure with the quiet, mellifluous instrumental interlude coming from the far corner.

"It smells like B. O. and nutritional yeast, right?"

Laney whispered in Clarissa's ear. Laney's boyfriend, Cobb, was up front swaying and nodding along. When they reached him, Laney dropped Clarissa's hand to whisper something into his ear. Cobb winked at Clarissa as he listened to Laney's proposition, then they disappeared into the crowd. Clarissa stepped into Cobb's place just as the song exploded and the crowd erupted into fists. In front of her was Jack Calvino, bent over and screaming into the mic.

Clarissa was enthralled, not only by the front man but by the fact the band was actually good. She stopped watching Jack to deconstruct what chords the guitarist played and how varied were the vamp sequences. She found that the songs were much simpler than her own, and yet sounded lush and hypnotic. She wondered if she'd ever be able to produce a sound like that one day?

The song stopped and Jack opened his eyes.

"Did I spit on you?"

She was distracted by snapping in the kitchen as two kids enacted the world's oldest mating ritual by chasing and slapping each other with their belts.

"Yot net."

"Do better next time, huh?"

A huge loogie flew between Clarissa and Jack and hit the floor.

"What the fuck?" he spun around and shouted. "Who is spitting in my house?"

Clarissa was surprised by the reaction and stepped back from Jack.

"Calm down, man," said the guitarist. "It's just wooden floors, we'll help clean up."

"Yeah, but there is still some asshole with a tired notion of what punk rock is disrespecting the show. Disrespecting us! Come on, asshole, show yourself. Be a man!"

The crowd up front split and a girl who looked like a *Les Miserable* version of Annie Lennox stepped up chewing a toothpick.

"I'm your huckleberry, bitch." she said, spitting the toothpick at Jack's feet.

"Come on, Kat—this isn't the Bowery in 1979."

"Oh, I know what this is...it's fucking boring!" And she spit again, missing Jack's feet by a millimeter.

"Why didn't you just say so, Kat. Shows over folks—Kat's bored." He threw the mic down and disappeared into the crowd of booing boys who fell in line behind the band and followed them outside. Clarissa glared at Kat as she settled into the drum set, rubbing her hands together while testing out the bass drum.

"What's your problem?" she yelled over the percussions.

"Did...did you really mean for them to stop?"

"Yeah, this whole scene is a sausage fest."

"The whole scene?" Kat began tapping the entire set in a 5/4 flurry.

"The whole fucking scene," she shouted. "Even the girls are dicks."

Laney and Cobb came out around the hallway, their hair mussed and necks bruised.

"What happened to the band?" Laney asked.

"I'll tell you outside."

At the door, Clarissa glanced at Kat to see her twirling a drumstick in her hand, stopping it in the middle of her knuckles to shoot Clarissa the bird.

"Watch out for flying dawgs!" she shouted.

"So who was that?" Clarissa asked Laney.

"Kool Kat. She goes to Monroe; used to be in A Poison On Her Lips until she and Jack broke-up."

"When was that?"

"Over Spring Break," said Cobb.

"Why did they—"

"Fuck if I care," Cobb said, lighting up a cigarette and smiling at the disapproving looks of the girls still standing in the corner.

"You care so much, go ask him yourself. That's why you're here, ain't it?"

"Well, I mean—." Laney leaned over Cobb's shoulder and leered at Clarissa.

"Shut up and strip."

"What?" Laney pulled her shirt off and wiggled out of her jeans and ran and dove into the pool. Cobb chuckled and flicked his cigarette to disrobe, and performed a cannonball that splashed Clarissa into drenching.

"Goddamn it," she tried to shake off.

"What's a matter, Clarissa," Cobb taunted. "You afraid to get WET! Are you Cinderella or Gizmo?"

She felt like all eyes were on her, but a sheepish look around confirmed no one gave a straight shit. No one paid her little group any mind—they were too busy wrestling and cock punching each other in the yard.

She pulled the damp clothes off and slid in to the tepid water.

"Head's up!" Clarissa looked up and saw a wagging dick attached to a red-headed boy with floppy hair and thick glasses. He leapt into the pool via the trampoline, and four more boys, equally naked, dove in after Ginger Warhol, and waterboarded him in the shallow end. Jack, still clothed, caught up with the ruckus and stood beside the pool to watch.

Laney splashed his feet. "Hey, Jack. I want you to meet my best friend ever, Clarissa."

Jack took Clarissa in. Although they spoke during his performance, Clarissa realized he was really seeing her for the first time—in her tighty whities. She wished she was a turtle so she could retract inside herself and drop to the bottom of the pool.

"We go to the same school, don't we?"

"Yeah."

"How come I've never seen you around?" he smiled.

"My...ah...mother doesn't let me out much."

"Much, or at all?"

"At all." Clarissa returned Jack's smile, but turned her face towards the sky so he couldn't see it. When she looked back, he was gone. The drummer dragged him away for something into the darkness of the backyard. His void revealed, through the window, Kat beating the shit out of the drums. It was an interesting beat, and Clarissa felt compelled to join her inside.

When Kat saw Clarissa dripping and transparent in front of the drums she stopped.

"You again. What are you suppose to be: a wet towel?"

"What was that roll you were doing?" Kat regarded Clarissa as she hit the drums again. "That one?"

"Yeah...it's cool. Could I...would you want to jam with me?"

"With you?" Clarissa nodded and grabbed the abandoned guitar. She plugged it in and dropped down to D.

Kat smirked: "Careful now, you wouldn't want to electrocute yourself." Clarissa closed her eyes and picked the riff she had made up earlier. She paused and waited for Kat to start.

"Okay, sure." Kat mumbled over the feedback, "Why the fuck not." She began the beat again.

As Clarissa had suspected, her song was made more boisterous from the drums—more lush, even. Kat seemed to think so too as she bobbed her head and mouthed a "fuck yeah" of approval to Clarissa. Clarissa paused to look for a pedal.

"Keep going," she shouted over the reverb, then found the pedal and jumped on it, shredding into the same riff, transforming the song from its twee arpeggios into a harsh heart-racing vamp. The euphoria of harmony and rhythm made her jump up and down, oblivious to all of the kids in the living room, until her guitar cut out and Kat threw down her sticks and started yelling. Jack and the other band members had them surrounded, and it was the guitarist who had pulled the chord.

"Goddamn it, Kat. Who said you could fuck with our equipment?" he shouted.

"Fuck your permission, Blake, you fucking fascist." Kat stood up and pushed the cymbals over.

"Not fucking cool, Kat. Fuck you! I hope you drown in a toilet when you O.D., you skank bitch!" The drummer yelled after her. She made to storm out of the house, and grabbed Clarissa's arm, tugging her so hard the guitar strap gave out and the instrument fell to the floor.

"If you knew the difference between your dick and a drumstick, maybe you wouldn't be so jealous, Henry!"

Clarissa met Jack's gaze as Kat dragged her towards the door. He wasn't angry and shouting like his other band mates, he looked…enthralled and a bit puzzled, just as Clarissa probably looked when watching him perform. Her legs jelly-wobbled as he waved at her.

Kat flipped them off one last time before exiting and yanked Clarissa aside and up against the siding.

"What's your name?"

"Clarissa."

"What's your deal, Clarissa?"

"My deal?"

"Yeah, you in a band or what? Where did you learn to play like that?"

"I taught myself. I'm not in a band...."

"You are now." Kat pulled out of her pocket a skinny Sharpie, and wrote her phone number onto Clarissa's captive arm.

"Call me tomorrow." Before Clarissa could explain that her deal made that impossible, Kat shoved her back into the pool and sprinted away from the house.

Clarissa gave into her chelonian anxieties and sank to the pool's bottom. Ignoring the churning and writhing legs surrounding her, she looked up at the sky. Through the water's waves and quivers, the stars shimmered like diamonds scattered onto black velvet cloth. She'd never seen the night sky before, not like this. The apartment complex yielded too much light pollution, and on a clear night, she'd be lucky to find the North Star.

The stars beckoned, and she floated towards them, pretending for a moment she was swimming into space. When she broke the surface, a bright slash scarred the sky.

"Hey, guys, I think I just saw a shooting star!" she looked over in the far corner of the pool and saw

Cobb and Laney were necking in the deep end. A pang of loneliness clouded her enjoyment followed by sadness that it was all just novelty.

She needed to get back home and check on her mom. Was she really still hypnotized, and if so, how would Clarissa wake her up? Did Clarissa want her to wake up? This had been the best night of her life, so far, and she wanted more.

Clarissa gazed upwards and recalled that you were suppose to make a wish when you saw a shooting star. She realized the wish had already come true, and somehow she had made it happen. All things happen for a reason, her mother would sing-song when Clarissa worried over things she couldn't control.

She checked her arm to make sure Kat's number hadn't washed off in the pool. Her mother could stay hypnotized for one more day. Probably do her good—allow her to rest free of pain and worry. And while she was resting, Clarissa could call Kat.

PART TWO

For three months, I have been caught inside one of those nightmares where you cannot awake. You hear and sense an omnipotent and ominous presence pursuing you, something that wants to do you harm. When you try to run away, you find your arms and legs are leaden, your eyelids are sewn shut, and all you can do is moan against the plight. I feel this doom until I am summoned, and when I am commanded to return to sleep, the terror pursues.

None of this is unusual. I used to have dreams like that all the time. It always involved you being in trouble, and needing rescue, and I never could get there fast enough.

But this isn't lucid dreaming, this isn't a nightmare in which I can't awake, but a gone body in which I cannot be gone. This is another kind of state in which I can no longer control you or what happens to you, you can only control me.

This is our new existence; it only resembles the same: "Mother, cook dinner," propels the body to prepare food; "Mother, let's watch television," propels the body to sit next to you on the couch, but I cannot inquire into your day; "Mother, take out the trash," compels the body to clean and walk as far as the dumpster, but it is difficult; "Mother, go clean yourself" compels the body to wash itself from soiling. It has been voiding all inner substances but soul—which rattles around the body like an ossified brain tumor in an ancient skull. "Mother, give me a hug," propels the body to embrace, but you haven't ordered that one yet. Perhaps because you suspect that the affections from a corpse are as bloodless and cold as the corpse itself. The body isn't your mother anymore, it is an automaton.

When the automaton has done her duties, it is shunned. You are gone on evenings and the weekends, perhaps in retribution for having to take on the adult things the body cannot muster. "Mother, sign this" propels the body to sign checks, but you have to mail and organize the bills. You somehow go to the store. Have you learned to budget? I can no longer produce a paycheck, no matter the command. All these things you must be doing, for you haven't seemed to have one problem that has made you miss your mother so much you wanted to talk to her and seek her counsel. I can't see or feel you—only hear you. And more often than not, all I sense is absence. As long as you command me, I know you are near.

Chapter Three

Clarissa sat in the backseat of Laney's car staring at the back of Laney and Cobb's head. They both chatted enthusiastically about something, but all Clarissa could hear was the radio. She looked out of the window, but it was already dark and the forest blurred with the road and sky, so she just stared at her lap and tried not to talk herself out of performing.

"Clarissa!" She jerked her head up to see Laney considering her in the rear-view mirror. "You nervous?"

Clarissa nodded her head. Laney turned down the radio.

"I feel like I might puke. Either now, or worse yet, on stage. Oh my God, what if I hurl on stage?"

Cobb turned in his seat.

"Dude, there's no stage."

"Oh," Clarissa blushed.

"Listen," said Laney. "First of all, this is the first time I've seen you all summer, so I'm assuming you've been practicing your little heart out. Practice makes perfect. You'll be perfect."

"Thanks," Clarissa muttered.

"I was kind of surprised you called. I figured you

either died, or didn't like me anymore."

"I've just been busy."

"Hanging out with Kool Kat instead of me?"

"Someone's jealous." Cobb cooed.

"That's what you've been doing, right?"

"If 'practicing with' means 'hanging out with', then yeah. Kat lives a block down and they have a house with a garage. We practice almost everyday."

"And that's it?"

"And mom stuff. Her work has dried up a little, and so it's harder than usual. I had to walk to a pay phone to call you. It's out."

"Seriously?" Clarissa nodded, and Laney grew quiet.

Outside the window, they sped past a cow meadow, and she saw the cows huddling together under a starry sky and a lone oak tree.

"So where is this thing at?"

"The Old Fields place," Cobb said, while digging into his pocket and retrieving a baggie.

"What's that?"

"Some old plantation. No one's touched it in years. There are shows there all the time."

"No, that."

"Anxiety medicine," Cobb smiled.

Laney hadn't taken her eyes off of Clarissa, and Clarissa met them, expecting to see her eyebrows cocked in devilish peer pressure, but instead they were serious.

"How is your mom, doing? I'm surprised she's loosened her leash for all of this."

"Her perspective changed."

"I'd say."

"What's wrong with your mom?" Cobb asked.

"Shut up, Cobb, and roll the joint already." Cobb put the joint in Laney's lips and lit it for her. After taking a drag, she nodded and Cobb took it and put it to his lips. They passed it back and forth, and Clarissa automatically rolled the window down to escape the skunky smoke dancing like Salomé before her nostrils.

"Does that stuff really help anxiety?"

"Yep. Makes the noise fade. You should hit it."

"Cobb. Don't. She doesn't want—" Clarissa yanked the joint from Cobb's fingers and toked hard, hacking all the smoke out of her mouth. She tried it again, taking it in slowly, and holding it in her lungs as she'd watched her friends do.

"First show. First high." Cobb high-fived Clarissa,

the first form of approval she'd ever enjoyed from him. Laney frogged him in the arm.

"Come on Laney, lighten up," he said, rubbing his arm. "I've never seen you be the serious one."

"First time for everything, I guess."

Clarissa sat back into the seat, and closed her eyes. She felt numb and tingly like her whole body had gone to sleep. She felt the car's velocity on the road, and imagined she also could feel underneath it the Earth's gravity. Was she floating out of her body? She opened her eyes to ground herself. *You have to find your gravity.*

More cow meadows, except under one oak tree she saw cows lying down around a bed. In it, she saw her mother, on her side under a pink blanket, but then realized when it moved that it had been a mauve heifer moon-bathing. Even so, she felt a twinge of guilt at breaking the ultimate rule in her household: no poisons.

"Jesus. I'm not sure this was a good idea."

"Just relax and breathe," Cobb said. Clarissa did the breath of trinity she learned from Dr. Gonzaga, and suddenly felt euphoric. She fell over in the back-seat and erupted into giggles.

"There ya go!" Laney cheered behind the wheel. "Let it all out!"

"Laney, you are my worst friend ever." Clarissa was too gone to realize her words came out wrong and had wounded Laney.

"I'm your only friend, bitch!" Cobb started laughing along with Clarissa, and Laney found herself chuckling. Before they knew it, they were on a bumpy dirt road in the middle of the woods.

"Oh, change it, change it." Clarissa scrambled up front to switch the radio station to the local public radio program, The Weekend Speakeasy. The Roaring Twenties ambiance filled Laney's Volvo as it Charleston-ed drunkenly in and out of the potholes. Clarissa sighed and stretched in the back, putting her feet on the window, and pretended she was in a Renault headed to good old Gatsby's joint.

"Man—I feel like Zelda Fitzgerald right now!" she shouted over the ragtime fog.

"What's Zelda feel like?" Laney's hands were keeping beat on the steering wheel.

"Exuberant lassitude!"

"No, that's called being high, you dork. Unless Zelda Fitzgerald is a kite, you ain't feeling her."

"She's feeling herself!" Cobb put his head in-between his legs and roared at his own wit. Clarissa continued to swoon in the back, and felt all her worries, including those that awaited at home, fade away.

The Fields plantation was a two-storied brick mansion with at least eight bedrooms planted in the middle of ten fallowed acres now reduced to a muddy parking lot. Russet bricks surrendered to invading battalions of kudzu and ivy, and the drained pool in the back was occupied by oscillating skateboarders. Inside, the tall ceilings and walls were decorated with graffiti tags of insults and illustrations of female anatomy. The shattered chandeliers strained upon frayed wires, threatening the revelers below. The mansion's centerpiece was a vast staircase where Clarissa imagined debutants once made their societal débuts. Now, their great-granddaughters leaned over the grand mahogany banister to puke with lady-like indiscretion.

Other than in the school hallways, Clarissa had never seen so many people packed into one place at the same time. She saw a lot of the kids from her school that had been at Jack Calvino's party last spring, but then she also saw a lot of strange faces. Kids from other schools, but also older kids, and cutting through the sea of crowd-mongers like Moses, was Kat.

"Oi, Clarissa! Where's your shit? We gotta do a sound check." Clarissa tried to gesture to Cobb and Laney behind her. Kat grabbed her face and inspected her eyes, pulling at the eye lids.

"Are you stoned?" she finally asked. Clarissa felt herself flush and wasn't sure whether Kat judged her or not. As far as she could tell, Kat was straight-edge, but she'd never claimed to be so.

"I got hotboxed," Clarissa lied, and regretted how easy that was becoming.

Kat shrugged. "As long as you can perform, I don't give a shit."

"No, I'm ready."

"Come on, then, rock star, let's show them what's up."

A strange thing happened while Clarissa was on stage. They were about the third band up, and for the whole show no one had been paying much attention to the music. When Clarissa and Kat walked on, no one took much notice, and seemed to talk louder when Clarissa mumbled into the microphone: "Hey. We're ah, we're ah Here and There. This is our first show."

Kat counted them down, and they began the set with a slow instrumental that did little to interrupt the cavorting. But it gave Clarissa time to get used to the crowd and to the microphone and the whole idea that in the next song she was going to have to scream and shout her guts out before everyone here and the world. It also gave her time to process that

Jack Calvino had just broke through the crowd to stand front and center. He nodded at her when she looked at him, and the belly-butterflies that had been smoked dormant an hour ago began to show renewed signs of life.

She looked over at Kat to make sure she was ready to transition into the next song, and Kat nodded. Clarissa turned on the distortion, and continued the slow song into a sudden loud frenzy making everyone jump in their skin and to attention. All eyes were on her just when she'd have to start singing.

Here goes...

People became enraptured with Clarissa's voice, and the harder she screamed the more they surged towards the stage. They played five songs total, each one more lush than the other. The crowd roared with applause and began shouting for an encore when they finished. Clarissa was stunned and looked to Kat for direction.

"Thanks, assholes, but we don't have anymore songs." Kat shouted into the microphone. "But we will. Here and There, and soon everywhere!"

Kat clapped Clarissa on the back.

"That was fucking awesome, Clarissa. You did great!"

"Thank you, and you too!" Laney and Cobb ran

up to Clarissa. Kat started disassembling her drums.

"Damn, girl, I didn't know you had it in you." Laney gave her a hug.

"Yeah, that was pretty good," Cobb said. "You didn't look nervous at all."

"I didn't?"

"No. You fucking dommed it."

"Thanks, Cobb."

"Did you see who was front and center eating it all up like a total groupie?"

"Yeah, maybe I should have spit on him? Do you think?"

Clarissa looked over her shoulder at Kat to see if she heard. Laney began cackling and stifled it when Kat came over.

"What's so funny?"

"Nothing. Just saying how shocked Clarissa's mom would be by all of this."

"Oh yeah? Why's that?" Laney smirked and looked off at someone in the crowd. "Never mind. You were great, though. You really wail the drums."

"Well, that goes without saying." Kat grabbed Clarissa by the arm. "Come on, stoner. This next band is fucking emo-wrist-schlitz. Let's go exploring." And before Clarissa could say anything else to Laney, including when to start heading back home, Kat dragged her off stage and away from the mansion.

"Watch out for groupies, rock star!" Laney shouted after them.

"What's a matter with you? You were real rude to Laney."

"That skank? I can't believe she's your best friend. She gets you high right before a show, then calls me a groupie when she's the one always talking about banging dudes." Clarissa paused at how off the wall and on the nose Kat was.

"She didn't call you a groupie."

"Then what was all that Jack Calvino shit?"

"I think she meant he was the groupie."

"What?"

"Like...in regards to me. I think." Kat stopped walking and turned on her heels to face Clarissa.

"Woah, woah, stop the mother fucking press. Jack would be a groupie for you?"

"Well, yeah, why not?" Clarissa felt a little insulted. "You had your chance, right?" Kat chuckled and started resuming her walk, twirling her wallet chain like Charlie Chaplin. "Well, well, well, Clarissa likes Calvino."

In the few months of burgeoning friendship, Clarissa never felt comfortable enough around Kat to ask her what happened with Jack. She didn't really want Kat to know she was interested in him even, for fear she'd think she was betraying their newfound sisterhood.

"Didn't you use to date?"

"Yup."

"What...what happened?"

"He has a wandering eye."

"What?"

"Like, seriously, he's wonk-eyed. It drove me nuts. You haven't noticed it?"

"Well, that's pretty...shallow...don't you think?"

"Calm down, Clarissa. I didn't mean to laugh at the idea that Jack likes you. Maybe he does, but I dunno if I'd take that as a complement. He is, after all, dating that Holly girl."

"The chick with all the colors in her hair?"

"Yup, Rainbow Blight."

"She's in my English class. She's kind of an idiot."

"Even so, they've been going out for a few months now."

"Laney never mentioned that."

"Sorry to break it to you. And I guess I'm sorry to

talk shit on your friend. Laney just bugs me, is all, and I just don't get why everyone likes her so much."

"Well, granted, I like her better when she isn't with Cobb. She's different when he's around. It's like no one else exists. But, otherwise, she's actually smart once you get to know her. Reads a lot, has great taste in music, and can even draw a little."

Kat twirled her finger in the air.

"And...she's helped me and my mom out a lot. Gives me rides everywhere. She's like my sister, you know?"

"Like your sister?"

"Yeah." Clarissa felt the sudden urge to go find Laney and apologize for dipping out on her.

"Besides, she doesn't like that I hang out with you more than her now."

"Yeah?" Kat grinned.

"Yeah, she gave me shit about it the whole ride here."

Kat put her arm around Clarissa.

"Well, that is good to hear."

"How did you get here, anyway?"

"My cousin lives out here, about a mile over there, so I'm going to stay with him tonight and he'll get me home tomorrow. If you don't want to get hotboxed, again, you can stay over, if you want?" Clarissa considered it for a moment, but thought of her mother. It was getting late, and she began to worry over what she might find when she got back. Her mother's incontinence was becoming more prevalent, especially when Clarissa went out.

"I can't."

"Suit yourself."

"I have to go home. Let's go back."

Clarissa and Kat undulated through the crowd. She kept being stopped by people telling her how awesome Here and There were, and had she not been panicking about her ride, she would have enjoyed it more. She stood on tip toe trying to look over admirers' heads to see if she could see Laney or Cobb, but it seemed they had vacated the ruins. Clarissa wandered into the valley of vehicles, and saw a big gapping space where Laney's Volvo should have been.

"How do I get home!" she shouted into the darkness. As in answer, she heard an engine roar to life, and a small, cyclopean light shone through the parking lot.

"Hey, that's Benny! I bet he could give you a ride." Kat began running towards her cousin, waving her hands and hooting after him. He pulled up next to them. He was a lot older—out of high school, and bared a feral resemblance to Kat.

"Benny, this is my friend, Clarissa. We're in the band together."

"Hey. Yeah, saw your set. It was cool. What are y'all doing now?"

"Clarissa wants to go home, but her ride ditched her. You think you could help her out?"

"Where do you live?" Clarissa told him and he whistled. "That's pretty far."

"Oh, come on, Benny. I can walk home, and besides, Clarissa's never been on a bike before." Clarissa regarded the machine skeptically.

"Fine, hop on. You haven't lived until you've taken a ride."

Benny revved the engine and released the clutch. Clarissa jolted from the roar.

"Shouldn't I wear a helmet?"

"Nah, we'll be fine." He held out his hand and she accepted, kicking him in the back trying to straddle the seat.

"I'll see you at practice tomorrow!" Kat shouted over the roar.

"So, what do I do now?"

"You hold on." He reached back to grab her arms and brought them around his waist. "Tight.

Like this." She felt weird hugging this beer-reeking stranger, but before she could think on it more, her stomach lurched forward and she held onto Benny's torso, cowering behind his back.

They left the Gatsby ruin behind in a miasma of dirt. She didn't relax until they were on paved road. She held her head up. The wind pushed into her eyes and nose at 40 mph, and she felt high again. Not the exuberant lassitude of earlier, but more active—more dynamic. All her worries swirled out of her lobes, down her throat, and emptied into the speeding air through joyful cries. With her head thrown back, eyes closed, she felt a sudden propulsion as Benny answered her laughter by revving the bike more.

The euphoria was ephemeral. The ride became bumpy when they hit a patch of bad road, and the front tire was not handling the potholes and pebbles well. Clarissa opened her eyes as she felt Benny decelerate. He yelled over his shoulder, but the wind grabbed his words, whirling them around and dropping them faintly against her eardrum.

"Hang tight, we're gonna crash."

Something inside her recoiled, making her body shrink behind Benny. All she could hear was her mother's voice repeating: *Over my dead body. Over my dead body. Over my dead body.*

The wobbling increased as he lost control and

wrapped the bike around a tree. Clarissa was airborne, and she gaped at the convulsing night, watching the stars sketched into lines by her shaking eyes until they were doused by sudden impact.

The sound of creaking wood awoke Clarissa. When she opened her eyes, she saw a thin pine tree fall over the wreckage. She gasped against the air like a drowning fish. Benny stood in the road, clutching his ribs.

It wasn't until she stood up that the oxygen found passage and soared down her throat and into her lungs. She was in shock and began walking towards town, leaving Benny behind. There were barely any cars on the road, and she stumbled in the darkness, feeling warm wetness dripping off her arms and legs with each step.

A familiar pair of headlights loomed over the hill, and once it had Clarissa in its beams, it decelerated. Clarissa heard a wolf whistle, and saw Laney hanging out of the window waving her hands

"Hey Zelda, did ya burn the place down, yet?"

The car pulled off of the road, and once Laney saw that Clarissa was covered in blood, jumped out before Cobb had come to a full stop.

"Jesus Christ, what happened?"

"You fucking left me. You left me all alone and I

didn't know what to do."

"Clarissa. Chill. We didn't leave you. We just took a walk, so to speak. We were coming back to get you, just now."

"How could you just abandon me? I don't know what to do!"

Benny came up from behind Clarissa and Cobb got out of the car.

"Hey, hey. I was giving this girl a ride. She's my cousin's friend...y'all know Kat, right?"

"I didn't have a choice," Clarissa whimpered.

"What happened? You drunk, man?" Cobb asked Benny. "Naw. Naw, man. Just a goddamn deer darted right in front of us. I swerved to not hit it, and shit...I hope she's okay?"

Clarissa was flabbergasted at the lie, but ashamed to realize that she had been the idiot that hopped on the beer-stinking dude's hog in the first place—because she herself wasn't entirely right of mind either. The shock shivered through her skull to her legs.

"You just can't leave me like that!" she shrieked before she fainted into Laney's arms.

* * *

You are gone. Where have you gone? Whatever threads keep me sewn to this body are trembling. The nightmare again. You are lost somewhere. You are hurt. You are scared. You have lost control. You've gone beyond the boundaries. I hear nothing but absence and I cannot move. There must be an ounce of will left within me. I must move. I must save you. You are my daughter. You are all I have.

I hear presence, now. Whispers and struggling and a door softly shut. I try to move my body. I command it, and I am ignored. I can hear you breathing and with that comfort I while away more purgatory with wonder. I wonder how did this happen? Did you do this or did I? Why have you let it go on so long? Why haven't you asked Dr. Gonzaga how to release me? For what good am I now?

I did not want to leave you, but in lingering in this shell, I did not know that you would will me to obey all the wishes that have gone against my own.

Over my dead body you have grown...you are much too young...but nonetheless, you have grown. You have to when you are on your own.

I hear knocking. I hear voices. I hear your voice. I try to move my body. I command it.

Chapter Four

There was adamant knocking on the door.

"Sarah! Sarah, open up. I gotta speak to ya. Open up, would ya." It was Mr. Argenziano. Clarissa opened her eyes, and found she was on the couch. On the coffeetable was a note written on a receipt that said:

"Are you ok? We should have taken you to ER but I know it'd get you in worse trouble than you probably are. <3, Laney."

Clarissa moved her stiff arms and legs slowly and hobbled over to the door. She cracked it open.

"What!"

"Oh ho, hello Cinderella. Did ya carriage turn to a pumpkin last night? Dance with the prince any?"

"What do you want, Mr. A?"

"I need to speak with your mom. Don't worry, I ain't trying to rat you out, although I saw your girlfriend had to drag your ass up the stairs and get you inside. Tisk, tisk—you ain't old enough to be drinking yet, are ya?"

"My mom can't come to the door right now."

"Yeah, yeah, I know she's sick and all, so why don't you take out the garbage for her every once in a while? There's starting to be a smell. Everyone's complaining about it." Clarissa sniffed the air.

"Maybe it's the disposal. I'll check it."

"Why don't ya go check it now and I'll go tell Mr. Tennant for ya. We can take care of the smelly business right now and do everyone a favor." Something down the stairs caught Mr. Argenziano's eye.

"He-ey, Clarissa! Who's your new broad?"

"Broad?" Clarissa heard Kat's voice.

"Shit," she whispered and closed the door. When she heard Kat hit the last step she swung it open, grabbed her and yanked her inside. She slammed the door and locked it.

"You never told me you had a resident guard-dragon. Jesus, you look almost as bad as Benny." Clarissa looked at her arms and saw they were stripped with jagged and bloody scratches. She felt her face and found similar lacerations. Her neck ached and her head began to throb.

"I'm okay."

"Did you go to a doctor?"

"No. Laney brought me home."

"What the fuck, Clarissa. You went to sleep?"

"I passed out."

"You probably were concussed. I can't believe that skank didn't take you to the ER."

"No, she did right. My mom would have killed me." Kat looked around and sniffed the air.

"Would it kill your mom to clean? It stinks in here."

"It's probably Mr. A out there. He seems to have smelt it first."

"Ha. What's the "a" stand for, Mr. Asshole?"

"Something like that." Clarissa stumbled over to the couch and collapsed. "What do you want, Kat?"

"I just came over to see how you were. To apologize, and to uh...make sure you and Benny are straight after what happened?"

"What do you mean?"

"Like...get the story straight."

The windows in the living room faced the other unit, and so it was a dark den during most of the day. Kat walked over to the lamp and switched it on, but there was no illumination. She pushed the switch back and forth, checked for a bulb.

"Hey, Clarissa, your bulb is dead." Resigned, she fell onto the couch.

"I don't understand what's to get straight. Your asshole cousin, bolstered by Milwaukee and machismo, took me for a ride against my will and we crashed."

"He said you hit a deer."

"We didn't hit a deer."

"No, you did. You can't be telling people he was drinking and driving, Clarissa. You are both okay, let's just forget about it and call it a deer. Okay?" Clarissa's head pounded.

"Fine. We'll call it a deer."

"Cool. I told Benny you'd be cool. Which, by the way, if you do decide to go to the doctor, he said he'd pay for everything. Just...let me know."

"Okay."

"And I have your guitar. The strings broke, though. If you got any spares, I can restring it for you before I bring it back."

"I'll come get it later. Don't worry about the strings."

"Well...like...are we still friends? Or, bandmates, anyway?"

"What? Yeah, of course. I just...don't feel good right now and want to be left alone."

"That's a relief, because I think we could win the Battle of the Bands next semester." Kat further surveyed the apartment. "This isn't such a bad place, but Clarissa, how can you not smell it? It's like rancid, dude."

"Maybe it's something in the garbage disposal. I'll tell mom about it later. Here, have a seat on the couch and I'll go get my strings." It was obvious Kat didn't want to leave without some sort of token that they'd speak again, so Clarissa acquiesced, despite how much it hurt to move. She'd never been in so much pain before, and she wondered whether this was how her mother felt.

The guitar strings were not in the piles of *Guitar World* magazines, mixed tapes, and used paperback novels that covered the floor. She began scattering the piles, uncovering nothing, and stuck her head under her bed to see if somehow the strings had been kicked under there.

"Looking for monsters?" Clarissa bumped her head on the edge of the bed, and felt of the already baseball size knot on her skull. Kat stood in the doorway, looking at the bare walls and magazine piles. "Woah, 1994." She bent down and picked up an issue. "These magazines are old."

"Yeah, my mom found them at a garage sale."

"Is your mom here?"

"Not really. No." Clarissa went back under the bed, and finally found in the far corner among the dust-bunnies the packet of strings. When she re-emerged, she found Kat sitting next to her, leaning her head against the bed frame.

Selena Chambers

"Listen, you don't have to pretend with me, Clarissa. I get it."

"Get what?"

"Your mom. No lights. The stink. My dad used to do the same before he split for good."

"Do...what?"

"Go on benders, disappear, and forget to take care of business. Whole time I was a baby, Mom had to like...drop me off at neighbors' houses—creeps like Mr. Asshole out there—while she went into town to try and fix things. It wasn't the best idea for me, but, hey, we do what we gotta do, right?" Clarissa nodded and Kat hid her embarrassment by picking up books and reading their spines.

"You really want to know what happened with Calvino?"

"Sure. I mean, no pressure."

"It was gross. Not that he's gross, just *it* was gross. Whenever we'd make out, I'd want to hurl and run away. And it's kind of just been like that with dudes."

"Maybe they're all just bad kissers. That's a thing, right?" Kat looked at Clarissa as though for the first time and smiled.

"Totally." Kat placed her hand on Clarissa's, and Clarissa felt her face flush. "They're bad kissers, and I never really dug them to begin with. I think I might

178

dig you though."

Before Clarissa could process Kat's meaning, Kat's lips were on hers. Kat sat back and stared at the floor. The kiss had been such a quick and tentative peck, Clarissa was unsure it had really happened except for a nagging tingle in her lips that telegraphed her brain to forget last night's weirdness, to pump Kat's hand, and lean forward for more.

She puckered her lips and closed her eyes. She could feel the energy from Kat's cheek tickle her own. It was all pretty romantic until Kat flung her hand away and screamed: "What the fuck is that!"

Clarissa looked up at where Kat was pointing and saw her mother looming in the doorway.

"Lisssssssssssa," she hissed.

"Holy shit," Kat scrambled to jump up, but Clarissa grabbed her by the shoulders.

"It's okay! Kat, look at me. It's cool. It's my mom."

"That's not your mom, dude, that's a fucking mummy." Clarissa's mother stumbled into the sole beam of sunlight in the room and she saw what Kat saw: she was emaciated and desiccated like the mummies you'd see in *National Geographic*. This made her eyes bulbous and her overbite protrude beyond her shriveled lips. Her hair was lank and limp, and her pajamas hung off her shoulder blades. Her bottoms had slipped off down to her ankles somewhere between her room and Clarissa's, and Clarissa rushed over to pull them up.

"No. She's sick, she's been sick for a long time. Mom, this is my friend Kat. Kat, this is my mom, Sarah Collyer." Kat stood up and approached them.

"Mom. Shake Kat's hand." Her mother's gnarled hand shot out and Kat recoiled from its stink before accepting it.

"Nice to meet you, Mrs. Collyer." Kat tried to drop the hand, but Clarissa's mother tightened her grip.

"Leeeeeeeeeave," Clarissa's mother hissed. Kat struggled to get out of the grip, but her mother bore down and twisted her wrist. "Leeeeeeeeeeaaaaaav-vvvvve Lisssssssa."

"Mom! Mom! Let go! Let go!" Kat was released. She scrambled and pushed Clarissa's mother out of the doorway and booked it.

"Kat! Kat, wait. Mom, go back to bed, now!" Clarissa ran after Kat, but by the time she got to the staircase, thankfully empty of Mr. Argenziano for once, Kat had already ran up the street and turned the corner back towards her house.

When she went back inside, she found her mother back in bed, eyes open and staring at the ceiling.

"She's gone, now, Mom. No need for alarm. It's just you and me, now." Clarissa sighed. "It's just you and me."

Clarissa watched what bit of sun sneaked into the room recede from the dresser to the carpet and under the bed until she was enshrouded in darkness. Kat had been right, her mother wasn't looking well. When she was up and about following Clarissa's domestic demands, she didn't look like herself, but some nameless creature that, only when it laid in bed, resembled her mother. Today, it didn't resemble her at all.

Epilogue

"Mom. Wake up, please. Something happened to you and I don't know if I can fix it. But I am going to try. I...uh...tried to find Dr. Gonzaga...but she's gone. Closed for business.

"I...think...I think you are still hypnotized and, at first it seemed good for you, but now...I don't know. All you do is follow my commands. If I commanded you to speak, could you tell me what's going on in there? Are you still there? Are you still my mom? Speak."

"Yeeeessssss..."

"Yes to what?"

"Yeeeessssss..."

"Talk to me."

"——didn't want you to know—afraid—it would—change things—it changed things—You— you are gone—Cruel—cruel—you shun me—in this bedroom—like—a grave—until you have a problem—only then—you miss me—you used to love me."

"Mom, what are you saying. I still love you."

"—it was too late—deflated—all breathed out— beckoning beyond—I don't want to leave you—you are still—just a child—mistake."

"No, Mom."

"—gone—must—save—."

"You can't save me, Mom. I'm growing up, and this is part of it. I'm learning to live."

"—I—am—learning—to die."

"What do you mean?"

"—I—am—dead—."

"Is it horrible being trapped in that body?"

"—I—watch you—grow up."

"No. No you don't. This traps me too, don't you see? We have to let each other go."

"—even—when you ask—me to let go—I remain—."

"You gotta let go, and I will try and help you. Be still, now. Be quiet. I think when I hypnotized you, something went wrong at the end and you didn't wake up. So let's try it again.

"Behold my pendulum, watch it spin as it calibrates the rhythms of our world. Right now, you are without by being within—you, too, must be calibrated. From the beginning or the end, follow your gravitation.

"I want you to breathe deeply. Slowly. When you

exhale, imagine you are blowing the soul out of your body. Now look within.

"Come back to the breath. We are going to breathe the trinity. Inhale through your nose until you feel it in your stomach and hold.

"Inhale now up to the ribs and hold.

"Inhale up to the collar bone and hold.

"Now release the breath through your mouth, and in that exhale, expel the fear from your body and from your mind."

"Ehhhhheaaaah."

"Good, Mom. Now repeat three times."

"—. —. —. Ehhhhheaaaah. —. —. —. Ehhhh-heaaaah. —. —. —."

"One more."

"Ehhhhheaaaah."

"Pain is only within the body. It distracts the mind and burdens the soul, sending the body into internal war. When you can master the body with the mind, the soul becomes strong and sempiternal. You have mastered the body with your mind, and unburdened by earthly pain, your soul will again reign. This is your last session, Mom, and when I snap to three, you will have found peace. I want you to awake, and I want you to let go."

Snap—

"Lisssssa"

Snap

"looooooovvvveee"

Snap

"Ehhhhheaaaah."

The Good Shepherdess

++May —, 1431++

My very dear and kind friend, the seignior and Baron de Rais, Marshal of France, the Maiden sends you her last final message via this courier, Jeudon. The Voices have told she with whom you fought in glorious battle at Orleans, Jargeu, and Paris that you have abandoned her to her fate, and that you believe the lies that the Maiden did not serve the King of the World, but a Dark Prince.

But what her inquisitors do not understand is that there are no Kings or Princes of this world; only the Great Old Ones who know nothing of Love, and only of Domination. And for France to remain free and pure from the British swine they control, Jehanne the Maiden had to give Him her soul.

* * *

The Voices tell me how to speak, how to move, whom to sacrifice. They have silenced my reflections, devoured my pieties, and possessed my tongue, forking and gilding it in blasphemies of our Lord and Mother. When my thought is effortless, it is THEIR thought. For my thought is…buried…buried under my service to them. They disguise all I say within semantics, and in an effort to protect me, make my meaning obscure. Unless it is about war—on that they have always been clear.

I used to be a pious girl; but what I have learned from battle, Gilles, is that our God is a delusion, and what we serve is more terrible than that wrath the Church teaches us to fear. There is no forgiveness in resurrection—only hunger, only servitude.

* * *

The Maiden knows why the Marshal flees Rouen—he saw things about the Maiden too terrific to explain to himself, much less before the Magistrate. The Baron's account is cast in a doubting veil leading to darkness. But the Voices have always shown the Maiden the way; and now they want to show you—who witnessed her fall thrice, and her rising thrice—they want to explain.

* * *

What I want to tell you is that I am not guilty of evil, nor am I guilty of miracles. I heard the call, it is true, when I was thirteen, when the stars sieged my family's pasture. It was dusk, and I was wandering back home after herding our flock to the next meadow, and I saw in the lavender sky several stars appear, twinkle, and then fall, their fiery tails whipping overhead and bombarding the field. One landed behind me, and I was taken under.

* * *

During Orleans, there was an arrow in her neck that brought forth little blood. While others around her grappled and died from their penetrating shafts, the Maiden merely snapped it from her throat, while still charging the Anglo savages, leading her flock to victory against *les Tourelles*. At the battle's end, de Rais saw nothing but a slight pink lump under the Maiden's healed neck.

* * *

I awoke face down in a water trough. My clothes were charred; my arms and legs were raw and red. My right leg dangled over the trough's edge—the bone snapped twain—but I felt no pain and found I could walk with the lame leg dragging in the dirt. I wandered homeward, passing scorched pastures filled with black-baked sheep, until upon a hill I was accosted by a robèd-priest. He held a spade, and when I tried to pass him, he raised it to halt me.

"Do you love France, Maiden?" he croaked. I struggled to ignore him, to pass by him as quickly as my lame leg would allow, but something within me seemed to burst forth:

* * *

The Maiden would die for France.

* * *

"What of your soul, Maiden?"

I succeeded in silencing myself, but this angered him and he grabbed my arm, clapping his palm right over a burn, but all I felt was the dull and slimy texture of his webbèd hand.

"Would you give France your soul, if you knew it would save Her?" I wrestled from his grip, but he held up the spade, and in the moonlight I saw my face—or what had been left of it from the starry blast. My long hair, uncut for twelve years, had been singed to the skull. How had I survived?

"Here Maiden, take this, for it is from The King of the World, who demands you do his bidding and go forth and fight. With this, you will live a thousand lives, and die a thousand deaths—you will be resurrected and live through Him, and in every battle you will be victor and all of France will be in your debt. Go to Glory, Maiden, go to Him. You can sit and weave wool

and bare children who will be captured and tainted by English blood, or you can go forth and bare arms and save all of France's children from tyranny."

* * *

Then there was the battle of Jargeau where after ducking a cannonball, The Marshall heard the cold crunch of stone against armor. The ball had stuck the Maiden's armored skull. She stood before him, her armor covered in British blood and her helmet dented where the cannonball had landed. She was merely stunned.

* * *

The monk pulled back his cowl revealing a round and noseless face whose amphibious features would have been disconcerting had I not been distracted by his pale, bald pate gleaming in the moonlight.

* * *

The Baron de Rais shouted after her in-between gutting a British page and beheading a fallen caval-ryman. He saw her take off her helmet, lick the flesh off her sword, and return the Baron's gaze, smiling and winking at him with the common bloodlust of friend-soldiers.

* * *

And that baldness was more than a naked skull— it appeared succulent, somehow appetizing—like a plucked chicken, a debristled boar, a sheared lamb, braised frog's legs. I knew he was lying to me about something, about his King of the World, about the War, and in my mind swam a drowning vision of a battle under seas, of gilléd-soldiers charging with our heralds, blue and gold, yet in the middle the fleur-de-lys seemed garnished with animated arabesques that reached up to me through the water trough I had awakened in.

I wanted to run from this man, return to the warm hearth of my family's farm, but the same instinct that forced my voice,

* * *

Hunger.

* * *

forced my hand into taking the spade.

* * *

The Maiden became hungry with the soldier's appetite—for blood and flesh sacrificed to the Mother Country, to the Dreaded Father. It was an appetite that appealed to the Baron de Rais, that allowed him to assist the Maiden and look the other way.

* * *

He was calling to me, Gilles, and spoke to me of life and death on this Earth, and spoke to me of our Mother Country, and how my answer would render me His puppet, and lead France and Him to victory.

* * *

Finally, running at top speed in a charge on Paris, the Maiden was penetrated again by an English bolt to the knee. Rather than topple like a hunted fawn, her pace was unhalted, the bolt unnoticed, and she out-ran the pages, splitting the skulls of several British swine in twain with her sword hilt, not once letting the Herald brush against the soil or become speckled with their blood.

Victorious at battle's end, the Maiden congratulated her soldiers and sent them to the farmer's fields to gather the night's dinner. She stayed behind, and knew not the Marshall tarried to inquire about the still protruding bolt in her knee. Before he could speak to her, he saw her sever and hold before her one of the split-skulls, which she shelled and slurped— like an oyster—the muscle from within. Then, hiding himself, the Baron de Rais watched her graze among the corpses, her cuts and lesions erased from her skin, and the precarious bolt pushed out from the bone and muscle, extracted from healing tissue, until it simply fell to the ground.

* * *

The priest knelt, placing his salient pate before me. He began chanting words from another time, another era, and while they fell on my ears foreign and brusque as English, within me the words translated: "Eat," he said, "For He waits—." Then he looked up at me teary-eyed:

"I am the good Shepherd;" he said. "The good Shepherd giveth his life for the sheep."

The Hunger then became overwhelming and I fell upon him and with strength never before experienced, I broke his skull. I pondered the grey oozing muscle—so this was what was inside mankind—and devoured it.

Afterwards, I looked at my reflection in the bloodied spade and saw my face restored. My leg was healed, my wounds sealed, the only remaining traces of my devastation were my ruined clothes and singed hair.

* * *

A Philosopher in Chinon once told the Maiden at court that scholars have always wondered where the soul was. He scoffed when the Maiden told him it rested in the mind.

* * *

I fled to the woods, and in an open field under the blinding light of the moon the Voices began. They began as one—the priest's voice spoke to me in a language not of this Earth, not of Christ's kingdom, and well outside the Mother's loving grasp; yet I understood, and they guided me through visions and instructed me on how to speak, how to move, whom to sacrifice, whom to save—all to ensure the Maiden would lead the Mother Country to Victory.

All one can do is serve—is sacrifice—a soul for country—.

* * *

They are to burn the Maiden at the stake.

* * *

I am relieved to go to the fire. To be relieved of these Voices, of these souls, of Him.

* * *

But be not afraid, Baron de Rais, the Dreaded One is calling, and he is calling for you.

* * *

I am the good Shepherdess.

* * *

The Maiden begs of you to build an army of souls for the Great One—and save all of France's children from Burgundy, Britain, and the Old Ones they serve.

* * *

The good Shepherdess giveth her life for the sheep.

* * *

Jehanne

Remnants of Lost Empires

"Mother, we travel together in our head where he hath given seed to see beneath the Aegean Sea and its still coolness. Below are buried cities whose absolute shadows fall above the surface as ruins."

So begins *Remnants of Lost Empires* (Der Drachenhaus Press; Berlin; 1809), one of the more uncanny volumes in the Starry Wisdom library. An apocryphal travelogue written during Romanticism's birth, it traces several ancient ruins throughout Asia Minor, including shrewd speculations of then unknown but now popular excavation sites like Hierapolis in Phrygia, the Halicarnassus mausoleum in Caria, and Constantinople's Sunken Cistern. However, most of the narrative is reserved for a series of visions claiming knowledge of earlier civilizations that the Greeks buried beneath their own acropolises. Most perplexing is the book's inclusion of several voices, the address of a "Mother," and the use of an arcane syntax resonant of Aeolian poetry.

While suspected by Classicists as a hoax, *Remnants* pioneered Miskatonic archeology, including first mentions of Hungary's Black Stone of Stregoicvar and Lemuria in the Pacific. It wasn't until this copy of the book was anonymously donated to the Church that new light was shed on the travelogue, making it one of the rarer relics among the collection.

This copy has added value in originally belonging to George Gordon, Lord Byron, who sent the book to von Junzt shortly before his death in Missolonghi. Included with the book was a cryptic letter, since lost, but copied by von Junzt in *Remnants'* endpapers:

"This book rec'vd with below from George Gordon, Lord Byron, on March 23, 1824.

'Dear Sir:

I have consulted with many scholars and all were nonplussed by its visions. An Athenian friend recommended that you would know what to make of it.

My interest is this: I believe I have met the author, who is not Otto Dostmann. Her name is Sarah Pickman. She is the "Mother," and she birthed this book behind closed eyes.

I met her during my first Grecian excursion. We discussed common sites visited—sites discussed in this book—but after our conversation, I realized that while we both had been to the Seven Churches, we had not seen the same places.

I felt like I had met an Oracle—she saw so far into herself that her mind transcended heaven and hell and everything in-between. Tragedy has led her to this transcendence. She deserves to be understood. I charge you to understand her.'"

Sarah Pickman (1780-1810) was an imminent member of London's cognoscenti, claiming friendships with early Romantics like William Blake and Mary Wollstonecraft.

A linguist, she translated the Greek poets, specializing in Aeolian Greek.

Her monograph on Sapphic cults caught the attention of the *Bas Bleu* society, who commissioned her to translate a (unsubstantiated) manuscript by Theodorus Philetas regarding fertility cults.

Intrigued by an allusion to Sappho in the scroll, she accepted the commission and moved to Paris. It can be assumed that her translation inspired *Remnants'* itinerary, but the tragedy Byron alludes to stirred the voyage.

Records at the Ipsalou Monastery, in the hills of Lesbos' Petrified Forest, confirms a deformed child was stillborn to a foreigner around the time Pickman began her travels.

This corresponds with the opening chapters regarding the island:

"The dawn and dusk skies are cirrus jetties of flesh and lavender reflected in the Aegean waves which echo the rolling Olive groves and Olympus and Lepetymnos' peaks. Using lava and earthquakes as their chisels, these rocky titans were Lesbos' sculptors. Some of the island did not survive the elements' distillation, and in the village of Sigri, a dead forest dreams.

* * *

Can you say the forest is dead? We only know the Gods through marble and stone—and we say they live. And from whose loins were they carved?

* * *

Kōma, Mother, Kōma! Here among the Gorgon trees, Sappho had her Cletis and taught the Vessels to love the Gods. Here, Mother was struck with me. The womb shifted—our minds are one with the soil.

* * *

This Forest also has a reflection. Beneath the soil, Time lays buried in layers to the Core. There civiliza-

tion begins. There stone trunks stand rooted and ver-dant—a bowery over the Unnamed who worshipped Those demanding filled Vessels to be spilled. Invasions and progress forced the race into the elements—into the earth, the woods, the seas—to only re-emerge in disaster and dreams. Their language remains etched in the wood beneath the glassy bark."

Whether or not the opening scene's eccentric dialogue can be connected to the mysterious birth at the Monastery in Lesbos, this beginning passage also sets the tone for the text's recurring metaphors and symbolism found among the ruins:

"The Sunken Cistern is part of a water reservoir network underneath Constantinople. Constructed by Emperor Justinian I, its huge vaulted ceiling is supported by 330 marble columns taken from various structures of the fallen Roman Empire. The arborous arcade resembles an alabaster swamp, the marble trunks standing in the still waters like cypress. Although they have no limbs or branches, their engraved decorations—chiseled tears and feathers—are the leaves commemorating the slaves and soldiers who uprooted and replanted these columns.

*   *   *

The Cistern drowns many things. At the northwest entrance, two Gorgon heads supporting the Northwest columns are revealed when the water is low. One lies on her cheek, the other on her head. They gaze away from each other supposedly dispelled of their powers, but perhaps it is to better guard us?

*   *   *

If the Sentinel Sisters didn't keep watch, the carp might sing forbidden lyrics through their gills, cease to swim, and begin to ascend the marble stairs—."

As Byron predicted, von Junzt was intrigued and his marginalia riddles the book. "Rather than write about dream palaces," he muses around the fifth chapter, "the author writes of resurrecting ruins like they are pruned roots that will grow back in full bloom."

After his own excursion to Asia Minor, he expostulates in a later chapter: "It is true that some of these ruins exist, but yet have others been found beneath them. Why does she write to herself through her unborn child? A hysterical hope that through these restored ruins he will bloom? If Pickman is the true author, did her translation transmute her body into a vessel that can't spill? What, then, was the key?"

Von Junzt's studies were inconclusive. His last entry, made before his death, concludes that the true answer probably lies buried beneath the ground somewhere in Anatolia with the other lost empires.

The Venus of Great Neck

I.

We worried for the Ellises. Twelve years ago, they—well, *she*, really—had been my dear friends. *He,* Hollis that is, had always been my competitor. But whether my personal preference was for Eva or Hollis, the point is they had left a myriad of friends behind them. They left the golden age of our youths behind when they stopped their parties and closed their gates to us. We didn't know why. I certainly had no clue. But sometimes, when I'd had more whiskey than soda, I'd wonder whether it had been because of me.

I remember towards the end, when we gents would retreat into the Ellis study to smoke, Hollis working himself up over alchemical mysteries and such, but Hollis was always arguing about some scientific postulation he was working on when he was in his cups. We'd indulge him until the scotch was gone, then one of us would turn the decanter upside down and say: "There's no elixir of life here, old boy."

Eva always rustled feathers with the other hens while they gathered in the drawing room because they'd inevitably resort to talking about child rearing. Eva would smile and nod while the others spoke of Little Billy and Jane's first steps and words, but she quickly grew bored when they all turned on her—the fox in the den—to convince her of all the parental joys she and Hollis were missing. Eva would mumble something about how fulfilling her sculptures were, and that Hollis was content with his work, so that the two had no room for little ones. But, when they looked back, some of Eva's lady friends felt that she crumpled under their last few taunts and grew more distant than usual.

But they always were a pair of birds. He was almost as crazy as she was. I suppose that's why she married him rather than me. My science was practical; I was an empirical man, especially after returning from the front. I wanted a family too, and a job that'd pay me to practice others' patents. Hollis was a mycologist and wanted to be the next Pasteur, so he spent most of his day among mold and fungi trying to cure the world's ills.

Eva was mad about her work, as well. She studied in Florence, stayed out of all that Modernist rot, and came back creating life-like sculptures that would have rivaled Bernini and made Pygmalion polyamorous. Commissions poured in from all over the Earth for her work. Baronesses and Ladies wanted to be remembered by their fading beauty rather than the angular wrinkles those modernists focused on, and would pay thousands to cross the Atlantic and sit for an Eva Ellis bust.

Yes, they were a bright, young successful couple, but many wondered if the marriage would last. The two were so pragmatic about their union that I spent a good deal of time mooning at a lake over whether Eva loved him or not, and whether she still loved me.

It didn't matter—when Eva loved, she loved freely. What Hollis thought of that, I never really knew. I assumed he ignored it, being occupied with secrets of his own.

*   *   *

It wasn't a sudden reclusion. The parties gradually grew further between, and the two couldn't be counted on to appear in public. I was the last to see them, a few months before they closed their bronze gates to us forever.

It was unpleasant. There was some unrest between them. Eva, looking sprightly with her new bob, sat on the couch sketching, trying hard to neither move nor catch Hollis's eye. Hollis, on the other hand, seemed more magnanimous than usual.

"You're in a chipper mood," I said, "Not so much, Eva, hey?" Hollis looked at his distracted wife, and smiled.

"Oh, Eva's ok. Just had a bit of a shock today."

"Oh, a bit of news then, Eva? Well, let's have it!" Hollis chuckled, and Eva's face morphed into marble. She caught, then cut away from, my eyes when her entire expression trembled. Her cheeks inflated, and she jumped up, sending sketches and pencils flying, as she ran out of the room with her hand over her mouth.

"I wouldn't say Eva considers it good news, old boy." Hollis met my gaze and held it while mixing drinks.

*   *   *

After that, Eva's telegrams arranging our usual rendezvous stopped arriving, and Hollis never called or invited me back to tea. I heard nothing for twelve years and was, along with all their other friends and acquaintances, cut out of the Ellises' life. Then one day I received an invite in the post.

"You are cordially invited to join Mr. and Mrs. Hollis Ellis on September 13th at 6 pm to celebrate the arrival of their greatest achievement and collaboration."

On the back, in green ink, Eva had written: "Your presence is *required*, my Mossy. Don't disappoint me." She didn't sign it. She never signed them.

A pair of birds, those two.

II.

They lived in Great Neck in a grand, gilded-age Italianate mansion on a hundred acres by the shore. I left the city at the same time as everyone else, it seemed, and mid-way through driving down East Shore, traffic backed-up. We all slowed into a pilgrimage caravan. We parked, one after the other, shook hands, and exchanged *les bises* as we walked in. Beyond those social niceties, no one spoke a word.

As we poured into the Ellis's foyer, servants helped us with our coats and cloaks and led us from the dark hallway into the bright chandeliered ballroom. A jazz quartet played demurely in the corner, and a banquet was laid out that rivaled anything Mr. Gatsby ever served up. A run was made for the champagne and cheese, and we allowed our unease of having aged and failed to be masticated and transmuted into a balmy-brained buzz.

With full bellies and bubbling souls, we chattered amongst ourselves about the good old days, then of the more recent days filled with growing children and dwindling fortunes. Eventually, conversation turned to speculation as we all exchanged rumors about the Ellises. Most accounts placed them abroad. Hollis researched some mycological miracle of ancient yore, where he stumbled upon some rare mushrooms with life-saving properties in Africa (or the Middle East, depending on who told the tale). Eva continued to sculpt, but no one knew what, as her commissions dried up along with their social lives. Others specified that she stayed home to work, while others claimed she mixed with Parisian occultists.

"Who, Eva?" I spat champagne. "Chanting among floating tables? I'd pay a pretty penny to see that!" More mulling, more munching, more rumor milling for an hour, until, finally, in grand fashion, our hosts appeared on the grand staircase. It was a shock to see how they had aged considerably: Hollis, once dark and strapping, was now ashen and gaunt; Eva—why, Eva looked like a sepia-toned wrinkle of her former self. The vampish bob had grown out into a matronly chignon. What had happened to them? Had we all changed that much? Withered or not, Eva and Hollis beamed and began greeting us as though time had unfrozen from 1929. When they saw me, they drew me into a sandwich-hug.

"So happy you came, Moss. Really jolly!" Hollis cried.

"Yes," Eva whispered in my ear, "It'll mean the world to her."

It's a funny thing when the word your ear has already filled into a sentence is replaced by one that logically has no context. Surely Eva meant to say "me," for there was no other "her" that I could account for wanting to see me. There was never another her, I wanted to tell Eva, but they flittered on clumsily and dustily like two moths diveboming all objects until finally meeting that great white light.

After the rounds, they returned to the staircase.

"Friends," Hollis shouted. "Welcome! Welcome back to our home. We have missed you all these years, but my wife and I stumbled upon a discovery that required our entire undivided attention. We have been working, friends, working hard on that discovery, which we hope tonight to share with you." He paused to look into his wife's brimming eyes. She smiled while grabbing the tear-vessel locket that hung around her neck. She flicked it open just in time to catch two single tears that rolled down her cheek. It was a rare occasion to catch Eva crying, but surely not so rare enough to warrant a memento. She closed it and nodded at her husband that she could carry on.

"This has been our greatest collaboration," she addressed us. "And so that you might truly appreciate it, we would like to take you throughout our home to show you our labors, our efforts, our life for the past twelve years that kept us from your warm company." The ballroom erupted into murmurs, and as the hosts turned to lead the guests through the house no one knew what to do but follow them stage left of the staircase, and go down into the wine cellar, now retrofitted into a laboratory.

Beakers, tubes, and the blue hiss of gas composed a still-life of the last twelve years. A funnel dripped a muddy colored substance into an empty wine bottle, one of the myriad unlabeled and spotless magnums that was eventually corked and stored upon racks against the walls. I noticed the racks, then the shadow cabinets hanging over them: all crowded by hundreds of fragile, crystalline tear vessels like the one around Eva's neck, brimming and Riesling-pale.

Powders were spilt everywhere, the glassware tinted and aged with whatever compound it had been cooking and re-cooking over the years. There was an open drawer and within it compartments for various bags of powders, all gradations of green, from the frostiest mint to burnt umber moss. The bags were nutty in that they had labels on them with names of objects rather than of properties: "SPANISH OAK," "BRICK," "DUNG HEAP," "BRONZE," "MARBLE," and "MINA."

What on Earth do you suppose a "Mina" was? You'd think they'd begin to explain it all, but all they said, all Eva said, was "This is Hollis's lab! He gets up to all sorts of hijinx down here. Pulverizing mushrooms and licking scraped lichen…."

It also seemed he experimented on marble bodies. In the far corner, on an anatomy table hued a dusty white, laid arms and legs askew from their torso, yet clinging to their core by ornate iron ligaments that laced all over biceps, triceps, breast, neck, and an open and faceless skull.

"Well, it looks to me like you're making a Frankenfop." Some of the party laughed, but Hollis stared at me, disapproving. Eva, recuperating a bit of her former self, smiled up at the ceiling. "Oh, you always dwelled too much on the Romantics. Bill thinks anyone with a beaker and a Bunsen burner is Vic Frankenstein." When the laughter waned, I walked to one of the tables and examined a pulley system rigged to pour the wine vessel contents over the marble. Veins and arteries of mold crawled over the various bits.

"Uh-huh. And, so, this pulley thing here with the bottle…uh…pouring over the …does what?"

"Oh that," Hollis said. "Simple really. Mold forms from moisture. A dead body exudes gases and moisture and is slowly replaced by mold—."

"Pore for spore, spore for pore," Eva interjected.

"Our theory is that the mold," Hollis continued, "in fact, contains our last essence. It's true for all organic matter. The mold creeping on the tombstone creeps on our bones, and all for what? So it can live. We die and it lives, and carries within it our life. Our project, a part of which you see before you, strives to reclaim the life essence mold takes from us and restore it." Everyone smiled and nodded politely, pretending it wasn't the stupidest thing they'd ever heard.

I stuck my finger in the over-hanging bottle and tasted it—saline.

"So you are cultivating mold on this marble here with tears?" I took an absurd stab, only to hit at the heart of their lunacy.

"No, not cultivating. More like summoning. That's where you all come in." News that we had a bit to play in this farce summoned mumbles.

"It's best not to think about it too much right now," Hollis chirped. "Come along, then, there's more where this came from."

We exited the lab through a door that opened on

to a courtyard. The cool air was refreshing, and as we winded the back of the house and crossed the yard to Eva's studio, I took a momentary solace in the full moon that broke through an ocular in the clouds. I thought about catching up with Eva, to whisper some stern nothings in her ear, but was afraid the conversation would only further emphasize the already increasing quirkiness of the evening.

Hollis grew increasingly giddy the nearer we came to Eva's studio, and it made the already bilious pit in my stomach more carbonated.

"Ah, here we are, folks," Hollis chimed. "Welcome to little Florence." The switch didn't work. "Hold on, wiring seems to be tapped." He walked over to a breaker and we were left inhaling the marble dust that hung in the air, hearing each other's nostrils rebel against the invasion.

After ten minutes, the studio blazed light into our dilated eyes. As our pupils adjusted, alabaster forms began to develop from the darkness. They were sculptures like the one previously seen; parts of wholes laid scattered about, being perfected, being molded into one lifelike likeness that had Eva's lofty brow. Other features seemed familiar, but I couldn't quite put my finger on who they belonged to.

Every age of what seemed to be the same child was documented in marble from infancy through adolescence—a pantheon of a growing child. Some were nude, but most were costumed in fashions from the past decade. The fabrics were all moth-eaten and mildewed, except one new dress on a dressmaker's mannequin made of mint-green silk. Some of the sculptures stood, some were frozen in dance with uplifted arms, and some laid in an iron-work crib.

Hollis let everyone take it in, and cleared his throat for what surely would be one of those obnoxious diatribes he used to give at the club: "This then, is Eva's lab, her studio. You already saw a bit of her labors in my sanctum. The marble is from Georgia, and is more porous than most marble, making it immediately susceptible to erosion and lichen. The minute the stuff gets outside, it sprouts!"

Hollis had a voice ideal for lullabies, so no matter how interesting his speech was, (and often it wasn't), inevitably your thoughts fluttered about the innocuous white noise of his baritone. So mine did, and distracted, I walked over to the crib to closer regard the statue baby inside. With its chiseled face covered in mold, it was not at all a sweet slumber, but a right terror, with pupil-less eyes that shun from the dark green moss ocular like two moons against a midnight sky.

"Why are you putting them outside?" Hollis paused from his speech.

"Ah, Moss, you have been most vociferous to-night. If you'll wait, old boy, I'm getting to that. Now, where was I?"

"Mina, dear," Eva whispered.

"Yes, Mina, and what all this is about." Hollis's blasé face became very serious and he gazed first at me, and then down at the mossy babe in the crib. "I was getting to that, yes." Then for the first time any of us could recall, Hollis was at a loss for words.

"That is Mina," Eva took over. "There and there and there. All Minas. All our Mina, our little girl, whom we lost twelve years ago."

She snatched at her neck looking for the tear vessel, and caught several rolling tears. She shook her head to indicate she could not go on, and waved for Hollis to resume.

"Yes, but only temporarily, you see. Eva has found a way to bring her back." A night of firsts, Hollis began to blush and act embarrassed. "But…we need help you see…that's why we brought you all here… need a collective."

"A séance, you mean?"

"That's it, Moss; a séance is just the thing."

III.

When we returned to the house, a stranger stood

atop the staircase. He wore a tuxedo and a black silk scarf wrapped around his entire head. He did not move, but cocked his head as we entered and raised his arms.

"Are we ready, Mrs. Hollis?" his accented voice reverberated through the ballroom.

"Everyone," Eva cooed, "This is M. Aubé-Gris. I am sure many of you know of him. He was in all the papers!" I had never heard of him, but whispers full of silly words like "mesmerist" and "spiritualist" flittered from lips to ears. To me he seemed like a Gilded Age magician, or maybe a Dadaist on a bad day. If his presence provoked anything in me, it was the begrudging realization that Eva had been up to something in Paris. Old tricks, it seemed to me.

The champagne had percolated into everyone's brains, and they grew giddy at the lark of a séance. M. Aubé-Gris raised his arms for silence and commanded us to link arms, clear our minds, and bow our heads. A muffled chant filled the ballroom— something like Latin, possibly Old French—. The more M. Aubé-Gris sang, the louder and clearer it became until I sensed he was shouting in my ear. I peeked at him and saw the black silk scarf swirling around his face and head, uncovering his mouth and obscuring his nose and eyes until it knotted itself around his forehead.

"Neat trick," I mumbled. I felt a kick in my shin, and saw Hollis—the veritable hawk to my squirrel—scowling at me.

"You are going to spoil it, old sport," he whispered. Aubé-Gris paused, then renewed his chant, and the scarf swirled back into his mouth until it suffocated his song into silence. He went stiff and still.

I raised my head and looked around, annoyed. Everyone obediently kept their heads bowed, their arms linked, despite a persistent "Pssst" from Hollis. Finally, I realized he was trying to get my attention, and when I looked up, he put a finger to his mouth, and gestured for me to follow him and Eva. I gave one last look to M. Aubé-Gris. He now stiffly held both arms out, and pointed north where Hollis and Eva were guiding me.

IV.

"What's all that with the scarf?" I asked as they led me outside.

"Ectoplasm, old boy." Hollis sounded somnambulant..

"Ecto, what?" Eva looked over her shoulder and winked at me.

Our destination was a mausoleum, which was absent from the earlier tour, and a structure I never recalled seeing on the grounds before. I know we were pretty blotto back then, but there wasn't enough methanol in the world that would have made me blind to this. It was made of the same marble as the child statues, and the door was cast from the same iron as their hinges; lichen and mold ran parallel to the stone's veins over the entire structure.

I never quite got the hang of the family vault rot—the need to have your own catacombs. Perhaps it's about convenience and privacy. Mourning can be an undignified business. But I'd much rather mourn and moon in an open graveyard where there's no chance of being cornered by a ghoul. No, no, you never knew what you were going to find in a vault, and if anything, the Ellises' vault was *a posteriori* evidence for my hypotheses.

I braced myself for cold, musty air as Hollis swung open the door, and was hit by heat and smoke instead. It smelled like a forest fire—half carnage, half rot reduced to black, ephemeral curls.

Inside was spacious, and lacked the usual bunk-bedded napping skeletons. In fact, there was only boarding for one here, in the oddest sepulcher I had ever seen. A huge oblong iron thing with three hinged-doored chambers. Wood crackled from the lower chamber.

The middle chamber was marked Whilamina Evaline Ellis, but bore no birth or death dates. Was this a sainted relation? I'd heard of keeping eternal flames, but this seemed dashed extreme. Even so, something about it compelled me to touch it, and I scorched my fingers.

"Eva, is this a furnace?" I saw her laugh on the other side of the sepulcher, and I realized that the top chamber was an open frame balancing a glass coffin trimmed in gold. Within the glass coffin was one of Eva's statues so overgrown with mold that the encrustation looked like an epidermis. The only places where you could see marble or iron were in the hands and feet, and parts of the neck and face. As with the infant sculpture that slumbered in the studio, mold surrounded its eyes like a Venetian mask.

The coffin was half-filled with Riesling-pale liquid that steamed and beaded down the glass sides. Spanish moss hair floated on top of the fluid, giving the sculpture the lifelike appearance of a bathing nymph rather than a boiled inanimate *object d'art*.

The decadence continued with three obelisks that flanked the entire structure. The two on the left and right each had concave handprint molds gilded by metal—the right obelisk had a lead hand and a tin hand, the left was poured of mercury and iron. The middle obelisk had another set of handprint molds gilded in copper and silver, as well as a gold-mold for the face.

Eva clapped. "Now, my dears, time is wasting! Hollis you are there. I'm here. And Mossy, you stand there." She pointed to the middle obelisk.

"And do what, exactly?" Eva ignored me and put her hands into the handprints; Hollis followed. He gave me a nod and closed his eyes. Eva did the same, which made me feel alone enough to join them in their stupid game and put my hands and face into the warm concaves.

Eva sang M. Aubé-Gris's strange song, her bathos inflections summoning within me all the pathos I had. I was overwhelmed by pity, sorrow, and confusion. They'd always been strange birds, certainly, but rather than that common strangeness bolstering each other, it seems they had worn each other down into total madness. Had she married me, I thought, she'd have been reigned in by now. But maybe not; back then, I just thought she was a fun-loving, good-time gal. Now that I had nothing to do in the gold mask but reflect, I realized she had always been dotty from the start. Maybe it was best things had taken the course they had…for me anyway. I'd never have been able to keep up, much less finance her idiosyncrasies.

Hollis harmonized with Eva. He was flat, which made Eva shrill higher. I sighed and stood with my face inside the gold mold, my steaming breath bouncing back into my face. With a bit of luck, maybe I'd asphyxiate and escape this occult escapade.

Eva continued to work herself up into a shrieking state, and then stopped, breathless. We waited for something, her gasps reverberating throughout the mausoleum like a clock—minute by minute, gasp by gasp—with no strike. Nothing happened.

"Eva," I mumbled from the mask. "Is anything happening?"

Silence.

"Eva…?" I stepped away from the obelisk, and wiped the sweat off my brow. I looked up to the ceiling, to the heavens I suppose, seeking soaring souls, or maybe black silk handkerchiefs, swimming through the iron ceiling to revacate bodies, but there was nothing. Just my two poor old friends hands deep into marble and madness, stunting their blooming future by shading it with the past.

The poor doll in the coffin continued to boil in tears, bits of mold flaking off and floating around like tea leaves. If only the fumes smelled of lapsang souchong, rather than scorched earth and veal. The whole thing was beginning to make me feel light headed, and I needed a reviver.

Even though twelve years had passed into utter insanity for my friends, I was certain of one thing that remained unchanged: there would be scotch in the study.

V.

I had to pass the party to get to the study. They were no longer paying vigil to M. Aubé-Gris' private performance and, undisturbed, had moved on to other follies. The band played "Let's Misbehave," and everyone charlestoned while throwing back champagne. Ah, the autumn of youth. I avoided their protestations and pleadings to join them, and beelined to the study. I poured generously from Hollis' scotch and sipped over my next move.

It seemed like a graceful exit was impossible. If I abandoned everyone during their ritual, I'd be blamed for its failure, even though it was all malarky and going to fail either way. I could just get good and drunk, and perhaps I could wake up in the morning with the guest's decency to pretend nothing happened. But, no matter how gone I got, I'd still wake up sober, and still have to look the Ellises in the eye and comfort them as they lamented the failure of an absurd and fantastical experiment, as though it were probable. Eek gads, they'd probably try and do it again after breakfast.

After my third go at the Scotch, I realized escape was the only way, and entertained how I could excuse, that is, whether I should excuse myself or just go. The scotch made me warm, but I was sure I could handle the drive back home. I could call a cab, I suppose, and arrange for it to pick me up first thing, "What ho, loads of fun Evie, but there's my ride. Must do this again…" I shuffled up to find the telephone, but before I could exit the drawing room, Hollis came in. He looked ruffled, his tie loosened, his hair mussed—like he'd been the victor in a mighty struggle.

"Join me for a tipple, Moss?" I considered my glass now empty of its third tipple and shrugged.

"That's swell of you, Hollis." He didn't look at me as he took my glass from my hand and returned it three-fingers full.

"And a toast is in order I suppose," he raised his glass. "To Bill Moss, mastermind of cuckoldry."

"Here, here, in your eye—wait, what was that?" Hollis downed his drink in one shot and slammed the glass down.

"Oh, in a way, it's ancient history. I've had time to come to terms with it. I don't think I'd be able to if she were my own." I didn't like the ring of his words, and considered them over a few sips. "But I thought twelve years of reshaping her, of Eva and I working to bring her back to life, would leave an imprint."

"Hollis. Would it trouble you to speak clearly just once tonight?" He opened his mouth to respond, but was interrupted by Eva throwing the doors open and swooping in, looking every bit the worse for wear as Hollis, but ecstatic and merry.

"She's here, Hollis! She's here." Hollis nodded and grabbed for the decanter.

"Yes, love, I was just mentioning that to Moss." She gushed and left us to return to the ballroom.

"Mentioning it? You weren't mentioning anything. You were speaking gibberish, like you've both been speaking all night, Latin and all. And that M. Aubé-Gris fella! Look, obviously something tragic has happened that has made you both daft. For that, I am sorry, but I'm dashed tired, old man. If you'll excuse me, I'd like to retire." With glass in hand, I began to break through the reconvening crowd, saying goodbyes and farewells. As I got through the middle of the crowd, I was stopped in my scotch-stumbling tracks.

"Wait! Don't go!" It was the tiny and uncertain voice of a child. I looked at the staircase whence it came and saw M. Aubé-Gris holding the hand of the statue from the crypt, all alabaster surrounded by dewy, fuzzy patinated skin. She was dressed in the silk mint-green dress displayed in Eva's studio, and her Spanish moss hair was swept up in a starchy chignon.

"Mina!" Eva said. "Everyone, *this* is Mina." M. Aubé-Gris released the sculpture's hand, and to astonished gasps and shudders, it moved. Underneath the silk sleeves, the shoulders and arms stirred like it was trying on the new frock of life. Satisfied with the fitting, it became animated, and ran down the stairs, rushing past Hollis and me, to embrace Eva. Eva erupted into euphoria, praising M. Aubé-Gris while holding the girl-thing out for motherly inspection.

By now, all gasps had been quelled by shock. When I looked at Hollis, he winked, and then I realized that this was all a joke—an elaborate prank on ole Mossy and the gang.

"Very clever, Eva," I bellowed. "I see among M. Aubé-Gris's other eccentricities he is a puppeteer and ventriloquist." I looked to everyone else to join in the amusement, but no one cracked a smile. They just stared at Eva and the thing called Mina. The Frenchman, meanwhile, frowned and shook his head at me.

"I'm afraid this isn't a joke, old sport," said Hollis. "It's a moment of truth. Eva'd never admit what I had always suspected about you two—that it wasn't entirely off when we were married. She swore the child was mine, and when we lost her, I decided to let it go. But, now, we'll see."

"Just wait a tick, Hollis; I resemble what you are

implying." The last three-fingers of his pour had soft-ened my mind and I felt the fool coming on.

"Indeed, Moss. Just watch." Hollis faced Eva and Mina with open arms. "Like this, M. Aubé-Gris?" The Spiritualist nodded.

"Mina! My girl! Come to your Papa!" The statue looked around sensing and unseeing, and shrugged out of Eva's python-like embrace. Without its ma-man's support, it wobbled in place, its arms swinging lightly on the hinges, its legs awkward under its own weight. It looked like it might collapse, but with a few unsteady steps towards the crowd, it found its footing and turned and trotted towards Hollis only to circumvent his grip to crush into me, ensnaring me in a spongy embrace. It was like being hugged by the bottom of the sea, and the little Galatea's arms squeezed the breath out of me.

"What's this, then?" I held my hands out, afraid to touch Mina, but then instinct tricked me when my glass slipped and in effort to catch it, I touched the slimy carpet of its neck.

"Father!" Mina nuzzled further into my arms. Hollis stared at me, smug and contemptuous. I looked at Eva, whose tears poured off her chin, the tear vessel necklace forgotten and rendered needless by the night's success. "Father! Father! Father!" Eva walked over and began stroking the sculptural child's

Spanish moss head.

"Isn't she lovely, Mossy! She has your mother's nose."

"Yeah, she's a regular *Venus de Great Neck*."

Its fuzzy face looked up at me with carved, vacant pupils. Then I began to recognize what had seemed vaguely familiar in all of the sculptures' faces. Jutting from the lichen was, indeed, my mother's nose, and I began to see my father's chin, both features that had been passed on to yours truly.

"Eva! Why...?"

She sniffed a few times, and then shook her head.

"No point, really."

"Look here, Hollis," I began to struggle against Mina's tight clasp. "If you wanted me to come straight, you could have just asked. You didn't have to import some Parisian vaudeville act to make me come clean!" The thing called Mina gasped and let me go, and ran over to Eva.

"He's mean," the tin-vox said from behind its mother's skirts.

"Really, Moss, Eva was right—you lack imagination, old sport."

Before I could further protest, Eva swept Mina up in her arms and they ascended the stairs. M. Aubé-

Gris followed, draping his arm around Eva in a way I didn't like.

"You call sharing imagination, hey, Hollis?" In response, Hollis ended the party by punching my face, and breaking my nose. The same nose inherited from my mother and passed to my daughter—the nose of the Venus of Great Neck.

Vintage Scenes #3:

Morellino di Scansano, 2011 Vendemmia

1. In a bathtub, fat plum-painted toes spyhop in steaming suds.

2. In the tub's corners, glass prayer candles flicker blessings over the water surface, transforming it into a scrye that not only reflects the little piggies, but the dour and emaciated faces of San Lazaro and San Judas Tadeo.

3. The toes belong to a tear-streaked, red-eyed girl sinking, soaking, and sulking sorrow among the Mr. Bubble fjords. She holds over the tub a half-empty wine bottle. She sits up, swings the bottle up for a swig, and let's it crash on the tile as she

falls back into the water, going under, holding the wine in her mouth.

4.   It is a Tuscan-something with a delicious but doleful taste. Black cherries, black berries, black currants, and black pepper—the four horsemen of the blackest nights of the darkest apocalypse. It has an abstract musk to match—like antiquity, like dust and cracked leather, dried roses and talc powder. It smells like Miss Havisham—like old people with dreams rotting inside them, or like the Coty lipstick the girl's Nana always wore.

5.   I keep saying the girl, but I'm the girl. I'm mourning. I'm drunk in the bathtub. Those little archipelagtoes belong to me and to my mother before me and to her mother before her. Those toes belong to Nana. Nana is nil, now.

6.   Nana liked to bathe us when my brothers and I were little. She would tell us to look to the water and tell her what we saw. I'd say: "I see Big Bird cracking babies like eggs and eating their yolks," a regular childhood nightmare for me. My brothers would see specters of the frogs and ants they had killed, resurrected and surfacing for revenge.

We were a ghastly lot, but Nana never judged or hushed our admitted crimes and fears. She would pull the plug, and sing "'Rub-a-dub-dub,/Wash it down the tub/It all just drains away!' There, my darlings, tomorrow is another day. We are all clean slates, again."

7. We were too young to think beyond ourselves, and so we never asked her what she saw and drained from her days.

8. In her claw foot tub, her feet stick out like flesh bergs in the water. Her life appears in ripples.

9. Between her feet: her visage appears young and blond, with pencil-thin eyebrows and spring-water eyes. She's riding on a school bus in a seat next to the dark, handsome, and world-weary driver. He keeps one eye on her and the other on the country dirt road. She looks out the window at a passing farm.

10. By her right knee: the man stands on a stage playing a banged-up acoustic guitar and singing into a Shure 55. Nana dances by the bandstand, hands up in the air, her skirts full with twirled air. The dress is made from potato sacks and full of patches. She is being watched by a cross-armed, static brunette wearing silk and lace and a gold band on her left ring finger that matches the one shining on the man's fretting hand.

11. By her left knee: in front of a parked 1939 Ford Deluxe is a chair cradling a swaddled baby sleeping in a makeshift nest of sheets and blankets. She and the man—now her man—embrace beside the display of their first born daughter.

   Next to the infant appears an identical chair with an identical swaddled baby, but the nesting is black and this baby is blue. She stands over it holding its hand, her face frozen in a Munchian wail.

12. From left knee down her thigh: a series of tombstones, some tiny and nameless, others containing siblings, parents, and friends. Most prominently is her husband, signified by a guitar leaning against the granite front, broken at the neck.

13. Around the Venus delta: the graveyard bottoms out onto a calm beach. She is alone and wearing a long, navy blue cover-up. Hunched over a fishing net, sea spray crashes over her feet and sand clumps fall from her hand.

   Her body has grown stout, her hair cropped, her face more withdrawn, and she looks over her shoulder wincing in the sun.

   And beneath her, beneath her outstretched hand, forms a frying pan cooking up mullet fillets. Around her feet are fish heads and viscera with grandchildren poking at the guts, scales, and innards with a stick.

14. The left thigh: her position is transposed, and now she is grey-haired and bifocaled, surrounded by lilac tile in a pink polyester nightgown, hunched over a faucet running water into a tub full of splashing toddlers. She is smiling.

15. I am smiling down at the girl smiling up at me. Not the girl. Not myself, even. Nana. Nana is smiling down at me and I smile up at her.

16. I am crying. My tears destroy the scrye.

17. Pull the plug.
    Watch it drain.

18. The wine is drained and the girl lets the bottle roll from her hand. Glass rattling on tile. Her tongue feels heavy and soft like shag carpet. Total blackness almost achieved.

    She leans back against the end of the tub and stares ahead at the feet that float like flesh bergs in the water. The fat plum-painted toes that spyhop in steaming suds.

19. The toes that are my toes are my mothers toes are my grandmother's toes, and they all curl together to slip down and enwrap themselves in

the chain hanging from the overflow plate. They yank the chain up with a splash and the evaporating suds swim towards the mini-maelstrom by our feet.

20. Rub-a-dub-dub
    Wash it down the tub
    And we all go down the drain
    When we pull the plug.

The Neurastheniac

The following excerpt is republished with permission from The Surhistory Dossier, *catalogued by The Bas Bleu Sisterhood in 2014.*

Helen Heck (1937-1968) was a poet whose incomplete and fragmentary unpublished notebooks, collectively known as *The Neurastheniac*, garnered her a small underground following as a result of bootleg circulation, most notably during the Nineties' golden age of the punk zine. Heck became most notorious when Boilerplate frontman Donald Lee made her last lines famous by quoting them in his suicide note, leading novelist Kathy Acker to write a small appreciation for *Vogue* magazine called "Lavender Slashed Wrists."

While she was a contemporary of William S. Burroughs and Sylvia Plath, and wrote of similar transgressive themes, she is considered a canonical nightmare and has been largely eschewed from any kind of academic or critical discussion for several reasons. First, *The Neurastheniac* is her only known work, and even then, exists only as a working draft. She never saw a byline during her lifetime, and there is no indication whether she intended the work to ever see publication. As a draft, it is raw and unstructured, and is at times completely incohesive and incomprehensible. It is because of this state that many critics dismiss it as an "Artaud-groupie playing in the Sanitarium" and often repudiate her accounting of factual events as pure fiction.

Even if it could be agreed that Heck was writing fiction, what kind of fiction is also debatable. Her work is highly confessional and lyrical, but her imagery titters over into high surrealism, and when her work falls out of its elevated strain for slang and simple language, it has the same spontaneous feel of a Beat novel.

While its literary significance remains in debate, her accounts of her Suicide Chambers trespassings are the only primary records known about the now demolished government building, making it a very important and rare historical document of a notoriously undocumented time, if in fact her account is true.

Staring Into The Suicide Scrye

Suicide is at the forefront of Heck's investigation and in the background of her life. The mid-ground was a struggle against the mental condition known then as neurasthenia and better understood today as bi-polar disorder. An only child born on a farm in lower Alabama, she came to New York City on a partial scholarship to Barnard College in 1955, and attempted suicide half way into her second semester citing constant disappointment in her surroundings, whether it was in Manhattan or back home, as too daunting to believe in a future. Having failed at death, she decided that Barnard was the better bet, and took advantage of the new policy allowing women access to Columbia courses. It is believed this is how she met the Van Dorens, who would provide tea and sympathy, encourage her writing, expose her to confessional poets like Robert Lowell, and introduce her to the Bohemian writers who hung around Washington Square Park.

With her southern accent, well-read wit, and sartorial eccentricities (she donned lavender sashes on both wrists to conceal her scars), Heck charmed the likes of Ginsberg and Burroughs, and while she felt a temporary affinity for their common interests in the occult, religion, mysticism, and mind expansion, a series of flings with other fellow intellectuals left her jaded and cold:

All the women here make poetry, while I write it like the men.

The women hate me and the men hate me and I hate myself.

The men who like me like me because they hate women and they can look at me and see themselves in a form they could fuck.

And so we all fuck and get fucked up and write and read and kill ourselves slowly by destroying our youth.

I can drink and shoot and snort and smoke all of them under the bed not because I want to die first but because I am the last to live.

* * *

It always begins with the ribbons—

Yank and tug like they're shedding Clara's corset in the garden:

'Why ya wearin' those lavender Chanel cuffs, bowed around your bones?'

'Because suicide isn't lady-like.'

To prove me wrong, for they must always be right, they kiss and lick the scars as though their moment of drunken Don Juan charm is better than vitamin E.

The admiration only opens new wounds.

When life is an orgy, no one hears your moans. (22)

An Existential Alchemy

What satisfaction Heck had came from her studies. At some point during this period, she found a copy of *The King in Yellow* in Columbia's library special collection, and began working on a thesis that focused upon the play's women Cassilda and Camilla. She theorized they were alchemical sisters and through several *danse macabres* knew how to traverse between the three worlds: the material, the after, and the imaginary: "It's an entire ether of the imagination and the collective conscious. It is there where Fates are made. The author of *King in Yellow* termed it Carcosa—if I had my way I'd call it Melpomene—and it is this dream-land the pallid Ladies reign, and it is over the entrance and exit to this existential twilight that they control."

From this connection, Heck theorized that the Queens in the mysterious occult play were of a secret alchemical sisterhood reigning over a realm that represented a mythical existence in-between the mind and the body. An existence she termed "the second act," and what we have termed the *surconcious*.

Her thesis was rejected as fiction and Heck ultimately flunked out of school and descended back into her depression:

Call me Helen—Call me
    Fuck-up and Failure—
Whose wasted vessel
Cracks ashore those
    Nician barks of yore. (57)

She burned the original manuscript, and the theories that lied within are extracted from *The Neurastheniac* and seems to have either provided the foundation or delusion for the visions she would have during her Lethal Chambers experimentation.

The Winthrop Government Lethal Chambers

If the gatherings in Washington Square didn't provide Heck with intellectual stimulation, it did introduce her to the abandoned Lethal Chamber that was part of the controversial Winthrop program of the 1920s. Opened on the south side of Washington Square on April 13, 1920, the Death Chamber, as it would become called, opened its doors to any poor sod who wanted to off himself. It was also the prototype for future federal death chambers that were to be erected in every major city and eventually towns. However, the initiative never went beyond New York City and plans for the Chambers were kept confidential, especially when the Washington Square prototype was privatized in the 30s. Shortly thereafter, the program was considered ill-conceived and closed in 1949.

"They found that given the choice," Heck mused in 1958, "more and more people chose to die before they even could live. It was the only choice that did not lead to more hydra-like decision making." (70).

Because the ornate marble building was also part of President Winthrop's Haussmann-like redesign of the city, and was intended to rival the iconic Washington Square Park in its flora, fauna, and fountains, it was condemned to decay and rot, and the name was changed to conceal its original function to the Wether-Fieber Hotel, and the Beats who congregated in the Park referred to it as the Hades Hotel.

It was from them that Heck learned the facilities' legends and became fascinated by a place where "you checked in to never check out. How did they fend off the regrets that weakens one's resolve? People warned me that perhaps the place was booby-trapped. One big ole mine or marble maiden....To enter into a building as beautiful as that, certainly the promise was to have a death of an exact pulchritude." (Ibid).

Heck began trespassing into the Chamber in spring of 1958, after failing from Barnard. Consequently, she began experimenting with opiates and other psychedelics, and would take an alchemical interest in mixing "cocktails" designed to "keep the mind elevated enough to find Melpomene. It's all fucking chemicals. It's all fucking alchemy. The mind has always been the philosopher's stone—the soul the e-o-l." (350). With each trespassing, interest in perfecting her cocktails increased. She became so enamored and convinced of her visions experienced in the Chamber, that she sought a "chemical change" that would allow her to sustain her residency in the dream-land.

"It was a challenge to the Fates," she wrote before her final vision, and it was one that she would lose.

Having spent a quarter of a century dabbling with self-destruction, Heck finally succeeded at taking her own life at 31 via one of her infamous opiate/psychedelic cocktails and a bullet to her temple. Her last rites, it seems, was to scrawl the now famous yagé-sipping bruja epitaph on every mirror, and shoot them one by one until the only reflection left in the room was her own.

Helen Heck is important to the Bas Bleu, even in fragments, for what may be her genuine exploration of the "surconcious." Whether or not the visions she experienced were in Carcosa or Melpomene is irrelevant—what is relevant is the mental map she explores, because it may guide us to the mental map within us all, and bring us that much closer to locating where the soul exists.

The following excerpts focus on Heck's exploration of the Chamber and the early visions that follow from her discovery of the execution machine. She never titled any of her fragments, and so all titles are editorial liberties made to convey a sense of time and development.

* * *

The First Trespassing

...was like a grand hotel, and explains the successful cover-up.

The Splitz-Carlton?

The Four Reasons?

The Callitoff-Hysteria?

Once you went up the bureaucratic stairs and passed Yvain's Fates, faces powdered white with bird shit, you entered Mrs. Havisham's lobby with:

• long mahogany tables full of molded and spoiled food rotting on tarnished silver platters.

• Empty chairs askew with broken legs and yellowed couches leered with broken springs.

• Floor to ceiling marble. Great Corinthian columns as wide and tall as red oaks. The aortal lines running through the flesh-colored stone gives the walls a sense of circulation.

• One large bay window—my light source in this

land of cut electricity.

- Frescos on the ceiling depicting some kind of afterbirth afterworld with three wet nurses delivering infants from cradle-graves and tossing them into the air like cherubs just learning to fly—narrative ruined by water damage.

Overlooking the lobby were the rooms. Doors ajar or unhinged. There had been a fire at the concierge desk:

- a cash register empty and charred—its gilding shining through the soot.

- Hooks in the wall for keys or hats.

- a leather-bound guest ledger half burned. A few pronoms still legible: Hank Mc———, Elizabeth Har———, Arthur C———, Meredith Jon———. Josephine Ch———. Lendell Beaureg———.

Behind the desk the drawers had been pulled out and also suffered torching.

Scattered on the floor are torched pamphlets advertising the special amenities of the establishment like:

"DIGNITY IN DEATH: Our PALLID MASK keeps one's countenance in place for a smooth, calm, and collected rendezvous with the Void."

On the front, a young woman with a Louise Brooks bob and a lavender tea gown wears a Louise

Brooks mask—cool, collected, and glamorous. Her eyes are closed, and the mask's cupid's bow lips are painted in a boudoir smile.

"LET THERE BE NO GRIEF: Full-cremation package spares your loved ones from material disassociation and financial burden. Includes cremation, ash disposal at a location of your choosing, or thousands of urn options for familial delivery."

And it showed a Valentino looking ghost hugging what seemed to be his living family...

* * *

Up the grand staircase. Extravagant for just one floor. Counted the rooms—grew bored at 50.

Each room basically the same. It was bigger than any apartment in the city I had known, and definitely better furnished:

- Elegantly furnished and draped in what was once reassuring colors of cream, gold, and mauve with rosewood furniture.

- There was a sleigh bed and a fainting couch upholstered in mauve velvet, now matted and worn. It lounged next to a Victrola.

- Victrola ornate. The horn made of copper, now patinated, and its cabinet carved in Art Deco geometries.

- Other flourishes of normality:
  - a vanity
  - an armoire
  - a personal lavatory with shower and bathtub.
  - a secretaire with unmarked stationary for any last thoughts.
  - a picked over book shelf—only had a copy left of Dickinson and Whitman.

I pocketed the Dickinson book and am taking notes on the stationary.

No windows, and in the waning light from the lobby, I tried to find the execution machine. No trap doors in the ceiling. Marble floor solid. I looked under the bed—nothing but monstrous dust bunnies.

Did the shower head produce gas? Or acid? Did someone come in the middle of the night and smother you with your extra down pillow? Room to room and more of the same—complete normality and not one sign of self-destruction.

Gave-up and started flipping through Dickinson. Music would be nice. Checked out the Victrola. Blew dust off the vinyl—Bessie Smith—and wiped it with my shirt to clear the grooves. Placed it on the neck and struggled with the crank on the side. Eventually wound the fucker up and I flipped the arm onto the vinyl. Surprised and relieved the needle wasn't dull. The Victrola's cabinet was also a lamp and radiated a warm white light into the room. This was alright.

I mocked fainting onto the mildew and dusty couch to read. "Because I could not stop for death/ He kindly stopped for me—." I couldn't focus. A series of designs began to dance on the wall. I looked at the Victrola and saw that its lattice work body was a zoetrope and the art deco octagons, rectangles, and triangles fox-trotted around me as Bessie Smith crooned:

"Noooobody knows you/when you're down and out/In my pocket not a one penny/and my friends, I haven't any."

Digging the vibe, I flipped through Dickinson and crooned along: "I'm noooooooobody, who are you?/ Oh, well, honey, I'm noooobody too."

Turned my tickle box over on that one, and had to sit up and put my head between my knees to stop and catch my breath.

The song concluded and the room was full of white noise from the continued fornication of needle and vinyl that masked a mechanical whizzing sound coming from inside the horn. I stood up and took off the needle and heard the noise more. I looked inside the horn and saw something gleaming down its throat, and stepped back and fell onto the fainting couch as a mechanical arm began to extend out and in its tiny hand was a syringe containing a golden fluid. I watched as it reached its full extension towards the head of the couch, and the hand depressed the plunger and the gold liquid streamed and splattered. Had I been reclining, as I had been before I lost it, it would have pierced my carotid artery. The arm retracted back inside the horn, and the dancing designs slowed down and faded as the zoetrope extinguished.

In the next room, the Victrola had an extra dusty Rude Bloom record. Same ritual as before and watched as the zoetrope shined through the cabinet to illuminate the room. I closed my eyes and let the lights dance upon my eyelids. It was soporific, but once I heard the mechanical arm, I snapped to and watched it repeat the motions of its brother machine: extend, inject, withdraw. However, after years of no lubrication, the arm did not completely return inside the horn. Before I could look it over, the Victrola lost its steam and I was cast in darkness. Had to use up my matchbook to see how to get out of there.

It seemed elegant but monstrous. The noises it made were un-settling and I couldn't understand how anyone would complacently allow the thing to penetrate their neck like some kind of robotic vampire. Were they sedated already before hand?

* * *

The Third Trespassing

Sauntering through the lethal gardens—
Once you hop the tarnished gates—
The grounds are so vast and brown
Shades of their former monstrous elegance.
Solemn stroll. Sobering stroll. With each
Step you become intoxicated by your
Next to last oxygen gasp.

* * *

A glance at
The shimmering fountain—a gaze at the
Rusted fountain—around its base hovers
The Muses.

I have met the Fates—.
I have met the Muses—.
Don't be fooled by what you can take,
It's all a ploy in their ruses—.
Find yourself with their golden nooses.

* * *

You can see in my eyes the stars
                    are gone.
You can see in my complexion the blood has stalled
                    within its constricted highways.
You can see in my mouth the lost words
                    caught in my teeth.

My dasein is perpetually weeping lactic acid
                    from the exertion to live.

And yet,

  by some involuntary propulsion,

    I move forward through the days and into

      the weeks and into the months—

For how long?

Alone, alone, alone. Alone with all the wrong answers.

    *   *   *

~~what is death but the failure to live~~

~~the secret in living is failing to die~~

~~what is death but failing to live~~
~~what is life but failing to die~~

the secret to living is failing to die

    *   *   *

"I have a world inside of me I cannot see,"
Said the oyster to the sea.
"I have resolved to shuck that little world outside of me."

    *   *   *

The Fifth Trespassing

I found a Pallid Mask and it is not as advertised. Neither the face of Louise Brooks nor any other human ideal. Made out of mercury with a silver arabesque around the brow and down the nose. An alchemical sign?

I reached into the Victrola and gently extracted

the arm. I rigged a fresh vial of morphine into the hand, and returned it to its cave, hearing its hinges and springs lock into place.

Cranked, needle flipped, and Billie Holiday's "Gloomy Sunday" filled the room. I laid down on the couch and placed the mask over my face and closed my eyes as the lux ballet began. The cold mask was making all thought in my temples frigid and frozen.

An arctic serenity in the igloo-skull.

The flickering lights' somnolent effect seemed stronger. With each inhalation I felt my body relax. "Gloomy Sunday" faded out as the beating of my heart grew louder and louder in my ears. A white heat pierced behind my ear—shot through with smack-warmth, numbed body—I became nothing but ellipses....

...Hugging the trunk of a giant weeping willow tree, the sun sparkling through its matron-leaf curtain dazzles me awake like a junky Snow White.

A garter snake coils around my outstretched arm and constricts it, above the elbow, to show the veins in alabaster. A hummingbird alights on my fingers and darts to hover above my inner elbow. It stabs its beak into my vein, hovering and sucking. The snake hisses in rhythm to the bird's fluttering and my gasping.

Eden ecstasy.

When the hummingbird is through extracting, it flits to the willow curtain and falls dead as if it hit glass. The snake uncoiled itself and disappeared in a hole at the foot of the tree.

Liquid gold pours out of my veins, and I crawl over to the dead bird—stiff and straight like a syringe.

I pick it up and crawl back to the trunk—nestle back in to its exposed roots and stab the bird's beak back into the vein.

Perdition Pain.

Gold spilling around the bird's body as I squeeze it, crunching the bones until all it had taken was returned.

Tapped, I throw the feathered pulp down and the snake emerges to swallow it whole—then disappears again.

I feel fortified and can stand and walk.

I part the matron-leaf curtain and look out over:

Nordic latitudes pause the rising sun—
Dusk is frozen on the horizon—
Casting the sky in jewel tones of magenta, violet, and
   aquamarine.

The clouds reflect these tones,
mix them with brooding, ponderous, slate precipitation.

It is nothing but landscape—
which changes with the journey—
It is impossible to survey and map—
because it only exists at the end of our threads.

The Fifteenth Trespassing

Who are all these people with faces and names?

They were my friends, but they are not the same.
They are not the same.

They wear their last suits and gowns—
          tweed, silk, chiffon, satin—
worth more than all the money spent on their minds
worth more than all the money spent
into their veins and arteries
worth more than all their lives combined,
if life were ever capital
to trade.

They were my friends—
      they were my lovers—
           they were my family—
These people with faces and names.
I recognized and unrecognized them
Their familiar faces wore unfamiliar expressions
Of last gasps—
cardiac cancers, automobile crashes,
undiscovered overdoses—
And faded beauties—
Entropy, gluttony, jaundiced, flaccid
Liver beauty spots.

These people with faces and names were erased
behind the masquerade of their own threads,
and looked out through porcelain hallows.
Each mask individualized by their individual demise
But made common by the same golden arabesque
that swept across the eyebrows and down the nose.
The secret code—the alchemical sign—that
Invites living specters to foxtrot at their own funeral.

They spin and twirl and jive
In their grandparents spats and stays
Around a grand table
That serves as throne and entertainment to
The two Sister-Queens—.
Whose corseted musculature
And golden-laced ligaments
And silk-skein tendons gory gleam—.

Their visages veiled in gold masks
Socketed with third-eye diadems of lazuli and tiger eye.

Cassilda wears a halo-collar that crowns her
Head in the warm embrace of Helios's arms—
Golden rays inlaid with rubies
and precious and imperial topaz.
Camilla mirrors her with Selene's serene beams—
Silver, sapphire and pearl.

They do not regard their subjects
They regard the marionettes on the table—
A makeshift stage for The Moirai—The Fates—

marble life-sized puppets trapped in a pantomime
by the Sister-Queens' gaze—.

*   *   *

It's an interesting tableau.

Clotho:

With bloodshot and puffy eyes,
Looks out a window with her hand
On the hip of her hourglass shape.
From her bosom and through her waist,
Falls infinite sand collecting at the foot of
Her petticoat. Her head tilts to consider
The long tapestry that is woven by Lachesis
And stretches toward Atropos to cut.
Clotho guides them to the hemming and stitching.

Lachesis:

With fair hair that rolls
Around her head into
A chignon of yarn; Pinned
By countless knitting needles
Of myriad gauges.

A lock behind her ear curls to her cheek
And she takes from it strands to knit
Into the tapestry.

Around her lithe marble body,
A spider spins and spins and spins

Confining her body to her chair
Only her arms are free from the
Cobweb garb, and she can reach
And grab from a basket containing
All of the scrolls—each a timeline of
Our lives—moving from one life to another
Under her sister's direction,
Without missing a click.

Atropos:

At the end of the tapestry, she sits cross-legged on the floor.
The murderer of men, her face is an open wound
From lacerations—the shark teeth tied
To the end of her matted hair—she shakes her head
like a gnashing rabid dog. Blood patina oozes from
damaged stone.

A string of black pearls chains her neck to the wall.
She wears a shawl made out of a fisherman's net—
Seashells, starfish, and rotting shrimp hang in the lapels—
Decayed brooches.

Ever ready in her hands are golden straight razors—
Once Clotho decides a life has ended,
She chops the thread with the velocity
Of a guillotine.

* * *

Atropos's arms flail at me.
She juts her knife at me—
            then at the projection on the wall.

The Sister-Queens' gazes go unwavered;
They take no notice of me.
I am just another reveler with a face and name.

I walk to the projection; grasp at the dust in the light.
The surface wavers and pools around my hand like
I had plunged it into a phosphorescent bay.
I felt minute pixilated threads stick to my phalanges
Like spider silk—.

In the projection, I saw myself—
A Helen who was not the fuck-up failure—
the windblown petals swirl around her face,
catch in her hair;
their vibrancy against her raven hues appear
as though her locks
Are wicks to blazing stars.

I look back to the Sister-Queens
And the incarcerated Moirai—

Clotho gestures to Lachesis,
who switches a thread between her fingers.
          The vision in the window changes.

Atropos juts her knife at me,
          then guillotines the tapestry.
She juts her knife at her sisters,
          and Lachesis searches for another scroll.
The puppets regard me regarding them.
Atropos juts her knife at the Sister-Queens,
          and then runs her razor across her throat.

Cassilda gestures to Camilla,
Who explodes from her chair
To rush and push me out of the way,
To make wiping gestures over the image.
The threads shudder and settle into a scrye.

I see myself in my last frock
And last face.
Flowing from the right temple,
Ribbons of Pink and Crimson silk
Layered with Grey and Aubergine lace
Enshroud a shattered and cracked
Porcelain mask—
All part of a cocktail hat
Composed of Cockscomb.

My eyes stare out of carved lids
Kohl-rimmed and mascara-streamed.
My sculpted lips are swollen
And smeared—
Nose and cheeks rouged by blood specks.

I touch the ribbons and lace
And poke at the Cockscomb.
My reflection merely scratches her cheek
With a shiny little gun—

I reach out to my reflection
She reaches out to me and aims.

I caress my mask.
The Sister-Queens bicker.

Camilla grabs my arm:
"You, madam, should unmask."
I refuse.
"Indeed it's time."
I regard my nodding reflection—
Her porcelain lips now carved around the revolver's barrel.

"You can't help but look out of the mask you were given,"
I tell the Sister-Queens.
Cassilda orders Camilla to unmask me,—
I slap away her privileged stretching arms
And rip the mask off myself—
The revolver goes off—.
....

The small scenes open up broader landscapes
        until various worlds
orbit around your eyes—
        Its induced vertigo—
And you hesitate where your next step leads—
        But you traverse—
You move on into Melpomene's weeping willow arms
        and wait.

For any minute now,
some soothsaying yagé-sipping bruja
will pass through this road-fork
                          and clear the cursèd humors.

Or maybe she'll just walk by with a dismissive wave,
laughing at the deer and snails in the sky.

Author's Notes

"Calls for Submission" is the desired refrain for all working writers, but in the circumstance of genre, the story itself must "submit" to certain restrictions and exceptions based on the publication's theme, motif, or tribute, not to mention the usual expected conventions of their market (i.e., horror, steampunk, science-fiction, fantasy). With the exception of "Of Parallel and Parcel," "The United States of Kubla Khan," and "The Last Session," all of the stories within this collection were written either for specific editors for specific anthologies or themed magazines. Despite the requirements of mythos and market, these stories refused to submit, and in their composition, I have held a conversation about another form of submission—the microcosmic horror of identity and existence, while exploring the more macrocosmic context of how identity can be lost within the negative spaces of history. By showing how these characters submit to their stories, I hope to also show the quiet and implicit ways they rebel—which is the case for most people who overcame their era—but were, for some reason, forgotten by history, or hidden within more famous shadows.

Of Parallel and Parcel

I began writing this in 2006, while I was working as a weekly newspaper reporter in South Florida. At that point, I thought it'd be a novel, but I kept writing off and on, and realized a year later that all I had were scraps. And, that isn't surprising, because all that survives of Virginia Poe are scraps. She is heralded in many circles as Poe's ultimate muse–the paragon of his Poetic Principle–and yet, her correspondence hasn't survived, and all we truly know of her are hear-says from Poe's family, friends, and contemporaries. Within some of these accounts are hints that Virginia was immensely smart and perhaps a bit conniving. Pair those minces with a quote I found from Marie Louise Shew, who nursed and painted the famous *memento mori* of Virginia, and as Carl Weathers says in *Arrested Development*, "you've got a stew going."

By 2007, I quit the newspaper gig, and returned to my much more affordable hometown determined to focus on fiction. But, I had to prove to myself that I could actually do it. I began drafting a new Virginia story with the above considerations and with a bit of Lacan and "The Purloined Letter," and over six months of doubt and hair-pulling, my story—her story—eventually emerged.

I emphasize the difficulty not to complain, but as an example to any new, aspiring writers who may be reading this. It took six months to shape "Of Parallel and Parcel" into its final form. That felt like a long time to wind up with just 1000 words, and believe me, I worried over being a "slow-writer" for many years after, but I learned a lot about how my brain pieces things together, and that has made writing a bit easier. While this was neither my first publication nor my first short story, I do consider this the one where I "got it." Where you wake up at 3 am with a refrain you scramble out of bed to get down, only to cut it up to pieces at 3 pm—and you hope the same phenomenon occurs again and again. I learned patience with the story, trust with the characters, and through them that the setting and period could be evoked without a lot of exposition. Having so little to work with, other than second-hand accounts of Mrs. Poe, allowed me to discover the delicate alchemy of imagination and fact needed to create historical fiction, get comfortable with putting words in the mouths of the dead, and to play with the subtler aspects of Poe's Ultimate Effect. And within all of that, the theme that runs throughout this collection began to emerge.

By 2008, "Of Parallel and Parcel" came into being. It wouldn't see the light of day until 2010, when it was published in *MungBeing* magazine's "Secrets" issue, where editor Mark Givens nominated it for a Pushcart prize. In 2014, it was reprinted as a limited-edition chapbook for Jordan Krall's Dunhams Manor Press. I am grateful to say, it sold out rather quickly.

The Şehrazatın Diyoraması Tour

This was written for Sarah Hans' *Steampunk World*. Published by Alliteration Ink in 2014, *Steampunk World* garnered some great reviews (EW.com, as an example) and won the Steampunk Chronicle Reader's Choice Award for Fiction. All stories had to be set within non-Western countries, and I chose Constantinople because I had already armchair traveled Anatola for another story, "Remnants of Lost Empire." I also didn't have to do too much research, as I'd already read quite extensively about Orientalism due to my interests in French art and literature.

This was my first attempt at writing science fiction and a proper Steampunk story. I tried to include everything I love and felt I had in common with the movement and also a few things where I differed. The love focused on how traveling has served two purposes for humanity. It reveals truths and knowledge of how we all live and exist, and it can conceal the same things. It's all a matter of where you look. Where I differed with the genre is that I have a more skeptical point of view of technology.

I wanted to write something that riffed off of mass culture—not just the stereotypes and assumptions the West had about non-Western societies and geography, but also how technology during that time could be used for entertainment and political legerdemain. Basically, I jumpstarted the difference engine with basic transhumanism as well as the more insidious elements of 2.0 social media. With the latter especially, I commonly bitch that people miss out on a lot of observational and experience opportunities because the world they build for themselves in their phone is more comfortable and full of dopamine.

Orientalism refers to the nineteenth century depiction of Asia, Asia Minor, and Africa by European artists. Thanks to the Napoleonic conquering in Egypt, France became the leader in promoting a stereotypical and exotic notion of these regions. Eventually, touring the Middle East and Egypt was no longer the purview of artists and adventurers, but became the grand tour for those who could afford it in the nineteenth century. This, of course, lead to a boom in tourism, especially within Constantinople.

Recognizing the economic benefits of Orientalist tourism, Sultan Abdul Hamid embraced it, and as his city modernized and Westernized, he sought for ways to accommodate the Western notions of an Orientalist Turkey. The train lines he established helped, but that was another modern intrusion into the Romantic Orientalist landscape. Always a man of his times, he immediately saw and embraced the propaganda potential of photography, and funded a great Photography Project that became the postcard image of fin-de-siècle Ottoman Empire. While this project not only catered to the Western expectations of exoticism, it also served as a global distraction from Abdul Hamid's political activities. The Library of Congress has made their collection of Abdul Hamid II's photographs available at their online photography catalog.

While it is probably apparent that this story was largely influenced by *Frankenstein*, there are a few major modern influences present in various ethereal forms: Jaron Lanier's *Who Owns the Future?*, a valuable tome about the integration of technology with modern life that ranges from transhumanism to surveillance, and Nick Mamatas' haunting Engles/Marxist steampunk story, "Arbeitskraft."

"The Şehrazatın Diyoraması Tour" was later reprinted in Hex Publishers *Words* zine in Spring 2016.

Dr. Lambshead's Dark Room

This first appeared in Ann and Jeff VanderMeer's *The Thackery T. Lambshead Cabinet Of Curiosities* anthology, published by Harper Voyager in 2011. The story was then subsequently reprinted in a Spanish translation for Josué Ramos' *Planes B. Vol. 2* in 2013. The idea came from the marriage of a concept I'd developed many years earlier, Poepathy, in a non-fiction piece I wrote for Philip Nutman and Anya Martin's *Up Against the Wall* called "The Poe-Bug" in 2007.

It was a creative riff treating Poe's long-lasting stature in the collective imagination as a disease; a notion that was actually inspired by reading the first Lambshead's anthology, *The Thackery T. Lambshead Pocket Guide to Eccentric & Discredited Diseases*. In 2010, I was working with Jeff on *The Steampunk Bible* (Abrams Image), and at some point we were discussing Lambshead, where I mentioned its influence on "The Poe Bug." Jeff was intrigued by that, and asked me to try and fictionalize the idea, involving the good doctor and myself. Since I suffer from Poepathy greatly, the story came about rather quickly and with much catharsis.

Descartar

This story was written in the summer of 2008, and had a long and arduous journey through the slush pile until it found a home with Jason V. Brock's *The Darke Phantastique*, published by Cycatrix Press in 2014. The original call that inspired the story was for *Haunted Legends*, edited by Ellen Datlow and Nick Mamatas. They were seeking modern retellings of classic urban legends. I went with La Llorona because I love ghosts that hang around water, and also because of her ties to lost children. It was my first attempt at a scary story, and I remember wanting to portray female body horror in a way that was authentic rather than what is often based upon some kind of predatory victimization by boogeymen.

The story didn't make the cut, and so it went the rounds for years. It was often rejected because one editor saw it as too pro-choice, while another saw it as too pro-life—which was interesting because I didn't see it as swinging politically one way or another, just a tale about how it went down for Remedios, and how it might go down for others in her situation and legend.

Vintage Scenes #1: Bandol, Château La Rouvière, 2002

The "Vintage Scenes" appeared in Issues #54-57,

of *MungBeing* magazine. They were to be a series published for every issue of the magazine's last year, but the idea exhausted itself by #4, and I retired the series. The first three appear in this collection because I feel they have a psychological and aesthetic unity that did not survive by #4.

My friend Stacy gave me the idea for this series during a conversation about the time traveling properties of a good wine. We could both remember what bottle initiated us into becoming winos, and what appellations could transport us back to Italy, Germany, or France at sip. I thought it'd be neat to write a few stories based on particular bottles of wine, and as a result, these became autobiographical synesthesia stories. #1 is based upon my honeymoon in Nice, where my husband and I did in fact participate in a wine tasting in the Côte d'Azur's oldest cave with some Australian tourists. Excepting that the narrator experiences the event of the story alone, it's pretty accurate to how things went down. The vintage featured in this story was the vintage I experienced in 2010, and it became my gateway to the romance of the vine.

Dive In Me *with Jesse Bullington*

This appeared in *The New Gothic*, edited by Beth K. Lewis and published by Stone Skin Press in early

2014. This is one of my favorites for many reasons, mainly that I got to write it with Jesse. We've known each other since small times and it was awesome getting to write about a world we both inhabited—deep south during the 90s—and rehash the spookier, more gothic aspects of our North Florida hometown together. I also really love the characters we created, and it inspired me to continue the exploration of that time as a teenage girl in "The Last Session."

If you like the deep diving aspects of this story, make sure to check out Jesse's weird historical novel, *The Folly of the World*, that takes place during the Saint Elizabeth Flood in fifteenth century Holland.

Collaborative Disambiguation *with Virginia M. Mohlere*

This was a prose poem written for *MungBeing*, Issue #12: "Collaboration." This was back in 2006, and I believe our editor, Mark Givens, paired us up. We wanted to write a remix of *Don Quixote*, but instead became each other's rock during equally trying times in our lives. I think we both were on the cusp of throwing in the writing towel, but thankfully we had this assignment to help us keep it together. As a result, we've been friends ever since, and Virginia is a constant source of inspiration. If you haven't had the pleasure of reading her work, go to www.virginiamohlere.com and do yourself a favor!

The United States of Kubla Khan

This story appeared in *MungBeing,* Issue #7: "Fanaticism" in 2006, and was my first major publication for anything. I dabbled for a while within Stuckism, Billy Childish and Charles Thompson's remodernist return to figurative painting. I tried to start a Florida faction in 2004, producing a single-issue online magazine, but eventually moved away from movement building. In this same issue of *MungBeing* are three of my Stuckist paintings. I also no longer paint.

I was inspired while sick at home and stuck watching CNN's non-stop coverage of Hurricane Katrina for a solid week in 2005. I don't know if it was the direct association with New Orleans, or just coming off of Nyquil, but I felt very zombie-like after watching all the reportage. I felt a disconnect that I'd experienced after 9/11, and have since experienced during subsequent national and international disasters. It's a helplessness unique to our time, and I think becomes fetishized and part of a national neurosis.

It takes a bit of abstract thinking to consider what is going on ten miles down the street, much less 400 miles, or 5000 miles away in the context of how you and it are interconnected in a cosmic sense. And the way we process news doesn't help expand the kind of thought we need for actual human empathy. So, the things we think we understand are based upon assumptions, and when you start to factor in mainstream media as the feeder of those assumptions, well, you've got a nation enslaved and crippled by Fear, as Dr. Hunter S. Thompson would have it.

Dr. Thompson factors into this story in other ways. He died earlier that Spring, and I started toying with the idea of a Dr. Gonzo-like lady reporter named M. T. Gonzaga who investigated and reported on weird legends and lore. This is the only story featuring Gonzaga directly, although I did evoke her briefly as the mesmerist that teaches the Collyers how to tamper pain in "The Last Session."

Vintage Scenes #2: 2010 Bernkasteler Lay Riesling Spätlese

This is another story closely based on my travels with my husband, this time along the Romantic Road in Southern Germany. I wanted to write a piece about locational mindfulness, how running up mountains suck, and the universal truth that Riesling rules. When I wrote this, I was missing Europe and missing the Florida beaches at the same time. You can't have it both ways.

The Last Session

This was originally published as "The Last Session: or, The Facts in the Case of Clarissa Collyer" as a limited edition chapbook for Dunhams Manor Press in 2016. It is a riff off of Edgar Allan Poe's "The Facts in the Case of M. Valdemar." This was a hard one for me. First, it wanted to be way bigger than it is, so a lot of time was spent cutting, cutting, cutting to keep it in some sort of short form category.

The material was difficult, as well. I began writing it somewhere around 2008, after my mother's own cancer went into remission. I finished it and had to work on proofs in the wake of my wonderful mother-in-law, Amanda Johnson, passing in early 2016. So, loss—both the fear and reality of—haunted this story from conception to completion.

Back in 2008, it was drafted as a police procedural, and was beta read by Jesse Bullington and Molly Tanzer. Molly had a great suggestion to flesh out the mother/daughter relationship, especially in the way teenagers treat, well, everyone. When I came back to it in 2015, I took those words of advice and ditched the police procedural and focused solely on Clarissa and Sarah Collyer, and loosely based on my recollections about high school during the rise of Emo.

The Good Shepherdess

This appeared in Steve Berman's *Zombies: Shambling Through the Ages*, published by Prime Books in 2013. This is one of those stories that languished for a while as fragments and notions. I don't recall what gave me the idea that Joan of Arc may have been a zombie, and I was actually more interested in her friendship with Gilles de Rais than anything else. The early drafts had him still solidering looking for her and being told to eat brains by hooded weirdoes. In writing that scenario, I realized I kind of hated zombie fiction. I filed it away until there was a call by Innsmouth Free Press for *Historical Lovecraft*, and recasting her and Gilles fates within the Dark Ones' shadow was what the story needed to be revised, tolerable, and most importantly, completed. Even so, it didn't make the cut until Steve was nice enough to give it a home.

Remnants of Lost Empires

This appeared in *Starry Wisdom Library*, a beautiful concept-anthology edited by Nate Pedersen for PS Publishing, released at the end of 2014. The conceit is that the book is an auction catalogue of all esoteric volumes housed within the Starry Wisdom Library—the archive used by Miskatonic scholars that houses all titles mentioned by Lovecraft throughout his mythos. Every writer was assigned a title, and mine was "Remnants of Lost Empires." All I had to go on was that it was written in 1809 by some dude named Otto Dostmann accounting his travels through Asia Minor. Because he had found something called a "black stone," the Miskatonic scholar Von Juntz referenced the source in Robert E. Howard's eponymous mythos story.

Nate had come across my "Wandering Spirits: Traveling Mary Shelley's Frankenstein," on WeirdFictionReview.com, and expressed an interest in a story from me that had the same femininity and romance. Given the publication year, I knew it was too late to involve Mary Wollstonecraft and too early to involve Mary Shelley. Given the source text's affiliation with Greece and Turkey, I turned to Lord Byron, and somewhere in reading it occurred to me he could have come across the author of "Remnants of Lost Empires," and that author was perhaps someone who was prominent during the time, but since forgotten to history. Usually, that meant a woman writer. Also tied into this is the misogyny present in Lovecraftiana...why were all the scholars men? Why were only men interested in the Old Ones? So, in retaliation to the Misktonic school, I created a sisterhood that dabbled in the arcane and esoteric, and the Bas Bleu were born.

The creation of the Bas Bleu has been a great

boon to my writing. Everything that I am thematically interested in—i.e., women in history, surrealism, historical fiction, conspiracies, alchemy—have come together, and I have been slowly working on a larger story involving them. Meanwhile, they have creeped up in other works. It is the Bas Bleu who rediscovered and preserved Helen Heck's notebooks in "The Neurastheniac."

The version that appears in this collection is slightly altered. Because *Starry Wisdom Library* was conceptualized as an auction catalog, each story featured a description of its book. Taken outside of that context, we were afraid it would seem random within this collection. I cut it from the story, but have included it here for any bibliophiles that might get a kick out of such things.

* * *

"Book's Physical Description:

—Cream calf leather covers with gold etching on binding. Pocket-size, measuring about 5 x 7 inches.

—Endpapers are blank (with exception of copious notes in various ink colors by von Junzt).

—178 unnumbered pages and with no illustrations. The book itself is quite plain and cheaply made, with the exception of the binding customizing the edition to be worthy of Byron's library.

—Spine is broken, and while pages 59 through 115 are loose, are still present in the copy.

—Contains an Ex Libris plate from that of George Gordon, Lord Byron, and is heavily dog-eared and marked in von Junzt's hand. In the endpapers is von Junzt's transcription of Lord Byron's letter to him."

The Venus of Great Neck

"The Venus of Great Neck" appeared in Spanish translation for Josué Ramos' *Acronos II*. It was published by Tyrannosaurus Books in June 2014 with plans for an English edition. However, that never manifested and this story appears here for the first time in English. This was one of those stories that was conceived for another anthology, *Fungi*, edited by Orrin Grey and Silvia Moreno-Garcia, but I was never able to bring it to closure in time for the deadline. It wouldn't be until a few years later, when I dusted it off to consider completing it for Josué, and viewed it through a different lens (in this sense, Dieselpunk lite), that everything came together.

At the time, I'd been reading through a lot of Prosper Mérimée, P. G. Wodehouse, Evelyn Waugh, and F. Scott Fitzgerald. Given the characters in this story are retired West Eggers, it is obvious how inspired it was by *The Great Gatsby* and it toys with the notion of resurrecting the past. The idea of the actual reanimated child came from Mérimée's "La Vénus d'Ile," which features a wedding destroyed by a vengeful, thwarted bronze bride. I didn't want to lay it on as heavy as Scott, though, and tried to capture the off-the-cuff tones I adore in Wodehouse and Waugh. I'm unsure whether I nailed that, but creating an alchemical chamber with a boiling real-life baby doll in it was fun enough that I'm not too broke up about it.

Vintage Scenes #3: Morellino di Scansano, 2011 Vendemmia

I liked this "Vintage Scene" because it allowed me to go and win a few rounds with Gertrude Stein a little, and it was a great exercise in syntax and style much needed at the time. It isn't about travel and it isn't as close to the source, autobiographically, as the previous two. I based the grandmother in the story loosely on some of my own grandmother's family photographs that I have in my possession. I also spend a lot of time in bathtubs seeking wisdom in bubble fjords, and as a result Frida Kahlo's 1938 painting "What the Water Gave Me" is one of my favorite images, and so I used it as the story's main visual device. There is some local color here, as well: the phrase "the blackest nights of the darkest apocalypse" is a nod to one of the most metal bands in all of my hometown, Spike Mott and the Blackest Knights of the Darkest Apocalypse.

The Neurastheniac

This story was written for Joseph S. Pulver, Sr., for *Cassilda's Song*, an all-female *King in Yellow* anthology from Chaosium. It was published in late 2015 and garnered a World Fantasy Award nomination for best anthology, as did "The Neurastheniac" in the short story category. While this story integrates aspects of Robert W. Chambers' *KIY* mythos, I strove to create a parallel mythos that belongs more to Helen Heck and the Bas Bleu Sisterhood because I knew I wanted to further explore both in future works.

When Joe approached me, he mentioned no one had really written about the Winthrop Lethal Chambers. Since 2012, I had been sketching Helen Heck and playing with the idea of a female bad-ass mystic junky that could hold her own with the likes of William S. Burroughs and Hunter S. Thompson. There were a few real-life models for her—Billie Holiday, Dorothy Parker, Kathy Acker, Sylvia Plath, Zelda

Fitzgerald, and Burrough's wife, Joan Vollmer, who Burroughs shot in the head during a William Tell game gone awry. While most of these women wrote about or performed their highly evocative modes of living, they all are recorded in history as victims or martyrs, and I wanted to reclaim them, collectively, as life adventurers like their male counterparts. Once Joe said "suicide chambers," I knew this was her moment to shine.

How, exactly, didn't come quickly. It wouldn't be until I was visiting friends in New York City, and we spent an evening wandering around Greenwich Village, that I realized the Lethal Chambers would have been built, and rotting in ruins, right across from where the Beats often gathered in Washington Square Park. Someone who suffered depression and had nothing to lose would seek that shit out—someone like Helen Heck.

I am "over the moon," as Joe would say, about how she's been received and supported. I can't thank enough: the World Fantasy Award judges for recognizing "The Neurastheniac," the readers who have told me how much they enjoyed this story, the reviewers who gave me much-needed shout outs, Chaosium for publishing such a beautiful book, and, of course, to Joe Pulver, who had my back from the beginning! Heck's adventures are continuing beyond "The Neurastheniac." As of the date of this writing, I am crafting a continuation of her exploits, more from the perspective of her cult following in the 1990s. We'll see where it goes.

Acknowledgments

If Hemingway was right about anything it is that writing is a lonely business, with a lot of time squandered within one's own skull brimming more with anxiety and self-loathing than profundity. The most a writer can ask for is to have someone waiting for them in the exterior when you return. I have been very fortunate to not only have my husband, Josh Johnson, to return to day in and day out for adventures and laughter, but a great gang of intelligent, fierce, and brilliant friends who make existential exigencies fun to explore since small times: Jesse Bullington and the Bullington family; Nicole Caputo; Raechel Dumas; Lesli, Stacy, and the Froeschner family; Bill Green; Orrin Grey; J. T. Glover; Charles and Karen Hill; Joan Horne; Sheri, Trevor, and Baby

J.M. Marshall; Brendan MacLeod; Aleks Sennwald; Saba Shariat; Molly Tanzer, Kyla Tew, and Nicole Wolfe. I wouldn't be who I am without the love and encouragement of my parents Joseph Chambers and Dr. Sonja Chambers, my brother Kent and his beautiful family Elizabeth, Stephen, Sarah, and Samuel.

Within the publishing and creative realm, I have also been very fortunate to find kindred spirits who have provided not only friendship, but mentorship and critical support by either publishing, beta reading, and/or supporting my work: Cheryl and joey, Laird Barron, Sarah Hans, Jason Heller, Jordan Krall, Nick Mamatas, MANDEM, Anya Martin, Virginia M. Mohlere, Scott Nicolay, Philip Nutman, Nate Pedersen, Diana Pho, Joseph S. Pulver, Sr., Ashley Rogers, Yves Tourigny, Ann and Jeff Vander-Meer, and Josh Viola.

In the above belongs Mark Givens, but he deserves a special shout-out. Not only did he give me my first break by providing for me and other artists a space to enjoy free expression, experimentation, and growth with *MungBeing* magazine, but he has always championed me, and believed in me enough to publish this book! Mark has mid-wived, nurtured, and helped me realize this collection in ways I never imagined.

Finally, I know how many books and stories

and words are out there vying for your eyeballs. You chose this collection, and for that, I am grateful. I hope you will continue to consider my work worthy of your bookshelf.

Selena Chambers,
Tallahassee, FL
January 2017

About the Author

SELENA CHAMBERS' fiction and non-fiction have appeared in a variety of venues including *MungBeing*, *Clarkesworld*, *The Non-Binary Review*, *Tor.com*, *Bookslut*, and in recent anthologies such as *Cthulhu's Daughter* (Prime Books, 2016), and *Cassilda's Song* (Chaosium, 2015). Her work has been nominated for a Pushcart, Best of the Net, the Hugo Award, and two  World Fantasy awards, including one in 2016 for the story "The Neurastheniac," included in this collection. Writing as S. J. Chambers in 2011, she co-authored the critically-acclaimed and best-selling *The Steampunk Bible* with Jeff VanderMeer (Abrams Image), but has since eschewed the initials. You can find out more at www.selenachambers.com.

AUTHOR SKETCH BY YVES TOURIGNY

About the Collaborative Authors

MOLLY TANZER is the author of the novel *Creatures of Will and Temper* (November 2017) as well as *Vermilion*, *The Pleasure Merchant*, and the British Fantasy and Wonderland Book Award-nominated collection-cum-mosaic novel *A Pretty Mouth*. Her short fiction has appeared in *Lightspeed Magazine*, *Nightmare Magazine*, and *Transcendent: The Year's Best Transgender and Genderqueer Speculative Fiction*, as well as many other locations. Her editorial projects include *Congress Magazine*, which publishes thoughtful erotica; she is also the co-editor of *Swords v Cthulhu* with Jesse Bullington, and *Mixed Up! with Nick Mamatas* (October 2017). She lives in Longmont, CO.

VIRGINIA M. MOHLERE was born on one solstice, and her sister was born on the other. Her chronic writing disorder stems from early childhood. Her work has been seen in *Jabberwocky*, *Lakeside Circus*, *Goblin Fruit*, *Strange Horizons*, *Ideomancer*, and *Through the Gate*. www.virginiamohlere.com

JESSE BULLINGTON is the author of three weird historical novels: *The Sad Tale of the Brothers Grossbart*, *The Enterprise of Death* and *The Folly of the World*. Under the pen name Alex Marshall he has produced the *Crimson Empire* trilogy; the first book, *A Crown for Cold Silver*, was shortlisted for the James Tiptree Award, and the final volume is called *A War in Crimson Embers* (November 2017). He's also the editor of the Shirley Jackson Award nominated *Letters to Lovecraft*, and co-editor of *Swords v. Cthulhu* with Molly Tanzer. He can be found in the Pacific Northwest, and more ephemerally at www.jessebullington.com.